THE GRIP OF GREED

THE GRIP OF GREED

NAVEEN KUNDRA

Srishti
Publishers & Distributors

Srishti Publishers & Distributors
A unit of AJR Publishing LLP
212A, Peacock Lane
Shahpur Jat, New Delhi – 110 049

editorial@srishtipublishers.com

First published by
Srishti Publishers & Distributors in 2024

10 9 8 7 6 5 4 3 2 1

Printed and bound in India

Contents

Author's Note

Before I started punching the keys, I had a vague outline of a story of two strong-willed women who go after each other. The quest for revenge often drives people to the extreme, as with Tanvi Mehra and Soundarya Kapoor. The unhinged protagonists who do not hold punches are often a writer's delight because, through them, he or she can weave a tale full of raw, intense emotions.

However, I needed a bigger canvas to tell the story. My inspiration was the Chaos theory—*the flutter of a butterfly's wing can ultimately cause a typhoon halfway around the world.* With that, I started developing a story to show how personal ambition and greed can trigger events that divide society and leave a trail of destruction and despair.

FLS provided me an anchor to develop a cocktail of politics and society. There is no right or wrong in the story or attempt at moral preaching. Each character has its own motive, which he or she pursues relentlessly. I kept the mood of the novel light and satirical because I believe the best way to tell a serious story is by making it not so serious.

I love all my characters, though my favourites are Lovely, Fattu, Kaalia, Toni, Moni and Dubeys. They were caught in the crossfire and selflessly take the story forward. I also like Heisenberg, but I couldn't fully develop his character this time. Maybe next time!

I need to acknowledge those who made the 'The Grip of Greed' possible:

A writer's mind is often plagued with self-doubts and anxiety. It was my good fortune to meet Suhail Mathur, who agreed to be my literary agent and took me under his wing. Since then, I have come to trust his judgment and value his friendship. Suhail—TGOG was not possible without you & *The Book Bakers*. Cheers to this and to many more in future.

Last year, I read the interview of Shri Jayanta Kumar Bose, the founder of Srishti Publishers, in which he talked about his journey and what Srishti stands for. His words sparked a strong desire in me to be published by them, and as they say, the universe (Srishti) gives you what you want bad enough, and so a year later, I signed a publishing contract with them. My utmost gratitude goes to my publisher, Arup Bose, Stuti, and Alisha, for all your work and support on this book. More importantly, thank you for welcoming me into the Srishti family with open arms.

I also thank Kaustav Das for giving me valuable suggestions as my alpha and beta reader.

I thank my family for their unconditional support and my friends for their encouragement.

Finally, thank YOU for picking up this book.

—Naveen Kundra
November 2024

Prologue

27 December

At half-past noon, the residents of Emperor Court and adjoining bungalows of Leafy Lane congregated at the pristine lawns of the Institute of Modern Arts. The assembly was scheduled for ten am, but it was two hours later that they trickled in their Jaguars, Maseratis, and Phantoms.

A fashion connoisseur could tell that most wore the latest haute couture. A few also brought their pit bulls and chihuahuas along. Everyone was told to get food, so the servants walked behind their masters, balancing boxes of sushi and salmon in one hand and silverware and crystal in the other.

The gentry mostly drank champagne, so a solar-powered cooler was installed at their assembly spot, and soon it ran out of space. Since it was a protest gathering, they wore black armbands with gold imprints, especially designed for the purpose. The flock had known each other for years, so there were hugs and kisses, and soon, some men were flirting with women, some men with men and some women with women.

There was a palpable bonhomie and festivity in the atmosphere that the organiser—RK Jain—an infamous middleman who had made the record of receiving the biggest-ever kickback in the country, decided to start 'out of worry' the proceedings before everyone got drunk.

He tucked the collar mike on the lapel of his Armani jacket and spoke in a harried voice, "Ladies and gentlemen, at the outset, I welcome you all. We are here to protest against FLS. Like all other government schemes, it is discriminatory towards us because they know we are not a big enough vote bank. We live abroad half the time and so, we don't get to vote.

"You may remember that a few years back, they brought in FEWS, and we had a similar protest. What good is FEWS for us when we have our own gensets and bore wells? We live in austerity and consume the least resources of the state, barring roads, which, if allowed, we can build on our own.

"We quietly suffered, but they have once again antagonised us by bringing in FLS. The time has come for us to express our displeasure and ask for our fair share. After all, we are the prime movers of this city."

There were a few disinterested claps from those who had half-listened. Rest didn't bother.

"I now hand over the mic to Malini *ji*," Jain said, reaching for his drink.

Mrs Malini was the author of the current bestseller titled *The Adventures of a Bored Housewife*. The book was likely based on her life, as it was rumoured that her husband was the chief accountant of a dreaded smuggling cartel and lived abroad. She was dressed in a satin kaftan, and a red *bindi* the size of a ten-rupee coin adorned her forehead. She was already three flutes down and was savouring the fourth as she slurred, "Fuck FLS. Just fuck it—" She wanted to say more but was too drunk to form a sentence.

Jain once again took centre stage. "We have learnt from experience that plain protest will not work. We will have to fast, like Guruji."

At this, a lady swooned, "Guruji, I love him; he is so sexy and what willpower. If I could do it, I would be size zero, and my husband would stop whoring around."

Jain was annoyed at the interruption but continued, "We have decided to do chain fasting. One person will fast for four hours, and then the next will take over. Together, we will shake the foundations of this government."

"Are liquids allowed in those four hours?" Someone asked.

"Only champagne," someone replied.

That brought a lot of cheers. The protest continued for another couple of hours. At the end, the wine cooler laid empty, and cigars and cigarette butts were strewn all over the prestigious institute.

***

The meeting at Model Cooperative Housing Society started at 6 pm after the folks had returned from offices and factories. The middle-class society on the city outskirts was inhabited mostly by white collared employees. It was a well-run society of well-mannered and disciplined residents who paid their bills on time, dreamt of sending their children abroad, and celebrated Holi, Diwali, and Eid together.

A *pandal* was erected for the gathering and the contract was given to Bholachand caterer for snacks and dinner. A separate arrangement was made behind the gym toilet for those who wanted to drink.

Mohan Khare was the society's president and took his job seriously. From morning to evening, he would inspect the common areas, which consisted of a 200 square metres green patch, two and a half trees, a fifteen-metre two-foot swimming pool and a half basketball court. He would get after the *safaiwalas* if any litter was found. He had retired after working for thirty-five years in a car manufacturing plant as QC inspector and had developed a passion for excellence and nagging.

The male protestors here wore unbranded jeans, sweaters and jackets, and women mostly *salwar kameez*, though a few were provocatively dressed in hugging jeans and even miniskirts. Every man, without exception, was leching on them.

Khare took the mike. "We are here to discuss FLS. I have been talking to you, and some of you support FLS, but most want the government to reduce taxes. That will put more money in our pockets. FEWS has been of little use to us because we consume more electricity than the limit under FEWS, and we hire tankers to meet our water requirements. They have to listen to us because we are the prime movers."

Khare's voice got drowned when the children cried with excitement as soon as the ice cream counter opened. Khare looked disapprovingly at Bholachand because this was planned for later, but the damage was already done. Soon, ladies got busy at the *golgappa* stall, and men slowly sneaked out to the gym toilet.

At 9 pm, the venue lay abandoned. They all had to reach for work on time the next day.

***

At 10 pm the same day, the residents of Karamdooma and Partapganj met at *Lal Basti* next to the city's biggest garbage dump. There was nothing to discuss. FEWS and now FLS were all they wanted. However, there were a few demands. They wanted the government to increase the limit under FEWS as most of them now had an air-conditioner in their houses. Second, they wanted the government to increase the quota under FLS so that they could get a mosquito-proof buzz.

But their most pressing agenda and reason for the meeting was to somehow evict Guruji from Azaad Maidan. His fast could lead to a complete withdrawal of FLS.

"Guruji is with the rich. Why is the old man having a problem if we are getting something free?" Hariya said after spitting out *gutka* on the primary school wall.

"Let's burn the venue," someone suggested.

"Only if government increases the quota. Otherwise, why should we dirty our hands for the government?" came a voice.

They were all seated around a bonfire in *kurta pyjamas* and smoking *bidis*. Most had tied mufflers on their head to protect them from the cold. Women had not been invited.

"Despite all these schemes, we have become poorer," a frail old man lying on the footpath said sarcastically. His voice was drowned, and he was shooed away.

"We have given our blood and sweat, and we are the prime movers of this city. We will not let Guruji decide what is good for us," an angry man said.

They shouted more slogans and, in a fit of rage, broke windows of a bus parked on the nearby road. Finally, it was decided that they would burn the protest venue at Azaad Maidan if the government increased the quota under FLS.

Rock Bottom

Two Weeks Earlier
13 December

"Is this the end?" She let out a soft shriek and curled her body in a foetal position as the tsunami of suicidal thoughts flooded her mind, plunging her into the depths of depression. In the ensuing hour, she tossed and turned on the bed, desperately trying to somehow block the onslaught. She went as far as googling her current state and trying the recommended quick fixes—silent prayer, positive thinking, meditation, deep breathing—but nothing helped and after every brief ebb, the pain made a comeback with a vengeance.

At last, she decided to suffocate herself to death.

She pressed the pillow on her face and counted: 1, 2, 3 ...

She had just started choking on ten when her phone pinged as a ray of hope. She threw the pillow away, uncurled rapidly, turned over and grabbed the phone from the nightstand, praying hard that it was a message from that one person, the one that could instantaneously change her circumstances.

> *Dear customer,*
>
> *Your EMI is 3 months past due date. We are forced to initiate legal action as per the terms of our agreement.*

Her hand trembled, and the smartphone slipped from her sweaty palm. Worse, it fell at an oblique angle, shattering the screen into infinite pieces. As she struggled to extend her arm to pick it up from the floor, her teary eyes fell on the dress lying on the floor under the amber glow of the rod heater. It was the one she had worn last evening. A glimmering red and gold YSL halter-neck paired with Swarovski crystals that she could ill-afford but had bought nonetheless for a very special occasion. Now, it merely lay there, limp and dead like an autumn leaf—a testimony of her failure.

As she thought about how her life had changed in a span of 24 hours—from heady euphoria to psychological lows—a steady stream of tears started rolling down her eyes and she once again grabbed the pillow to get on with the unfinished task. She may have succeeded this time if not for the WhatsApp beep, which resuscitated her hope once again. Mustering all her strength, she leaned over the edge of the bed to look at the phone lying on the floor. She could barely make out the text on the broken screen, but then, there was not much to read.

You were removed

That felt like a sucker punch and she closed her eyes and braced for another wave of nausea, but for some strange reason felt an adrenaline rush instead. It was as if the notification had injected serotonin in her bloodstream.

It was only later that she reckoned that she had hit rock-bottom at that instant. All her dreams had shattered, the years of work undone, but probably her removal from the group which she had founded was the final nail in the coffin that had emptied her bucket of sadness.

She no longer had the strength and intention to mourn. She had hit rock-bottom and the only way to go was up.

The path to paradise begins in hell!

She instantly knew her next course of action and, like a phoenix rising from ashes, sprang up from the bed with a calm and clear head. She went into the bathroom and smiled at her reflection in the mirror. Next, she threw the rusty single-use razors and empty shampoo sachets scattered all over into the dustbin and arranged the toiletries in a neat line. Then, with a great sense of purpose, she took a scrubber and cleaned the floor tiles, diligently removing dirt from the crevices. She opened the drain strainer and wiped it clean of hair and lint of all sorts.

Once she was satisfied, she poured a bucket of water on the floor and mopped it dry. She brushed her teeth and then stood under the ice-cold shower, soaking in the invigorating needles. Once back in the bedroom, she picked up the dress and neatly put it back on the hanger. She looked at the wall clock. It was one minute past midnight and the new day had started—the first day of the rest of her life!

The exhaustion made her reach for the water bottle, and it was then she noticed the person snoring on the bed. *Oblivious to my pain, the asshole is sleeping as if nothing has happened.* A wave of anger swept through her, and at that moment, she hated him more than ever. She knew he was dim-witted, but then everyone responds to physical pain. On an impulse, she extended her leg and gave a hard kick in his gut and shouted, "Is this the fucking end?"

"*Bhukump aa gaya! Bhukump aa gaya…*" He let out a panic-stricken cry and jumped from the bed while scrambling to pull up his shorts, which had rolled down because of worn-out elastic.

She looked at him and burst out laughing. Just the pleasure of seeing him shaken and stirred overshadowed her current state of depression, though only momentarily, as clouds of anxiety quickly engulfed her once again. Still, there was a tint of satisfaction. It was not that only others could inflict pain on her; she could also do the same to others.

"There is no earthquake. It would have been better if there was one. Switch on the light; we need to discuss something," she said roughly.

"Discuss what?" He rubbed his eyes and replied meekly.

"Switch on the light," she ordered.

"You kicked me, didn't you?" He said accusingly, then turned the switch on and the soft glow of the bedside lamp enveloped the room.

"You deserve a lot more pain than that…and for god's sake, change your fuckin shorts; you have nothing special in there that you keep displaying."

He meekly held his shorts in his hands and entered the bathroom. He came out a minute later with a towel wrapped around his waist. "What's the point of losing sleep over it? Let's wait for some more time. Maybe she will change her mind," he said with an inscrutable, calm face, though he was desperate to coax her to sleep.

Instead of softening, she glared balefully at him, "What kind of man are you? Don't you feel any anger…if you don't, you can go back to sleep, but the moment you do that, I will pour hot water on your deflated ego."

"As if that will solve everything," he mumbled, hoping a fraction later that she didn't hear him.

"You are too dull to feel emotional pain; at least when your balls are set on fire, you will feel something," she sniped back.

"What exactly do you want from me in the middle of the night?" He raised his hands in desperation.

"We need to plan and decide our next step, our counteroffensive. She is not the queen of Victoria who can ruin our lives on a whim. We have worked very hard, made sacrifices, have done everything for her, and now we can't let her destroy us. It's not only me, it's we," she deliberately emphasised *we* and looked at him with beseeching eyes.

"You are right, but I thought maybe we can discuss it tomorrow morning with a fresh mind," he mumbled.

She stared at him with cold eyes. "I am fed up with your pussyfooting. No, it must be done today, right now. By tomorrow, this anger will subside; maybe this pain will also go away. We must discuss things tonight. We will have to make some hard decisions. There will be sacrifices to be made. But ultimately, we will succeed. Let's have a drink and decide everything...wait, let's shift to the balcony. Get the bottle from the kitchen." She moved swiftly and covered her nakedness with an overcoat.

Fifteen minutes later, they were sitting on the balcony on a cold, starless night. The temperature was minus ten degrees and, despite wearing a monkey cap and thermal vest, he was shivering. She seemed unaffected by the weather.

"Where is the soda?" She asked, filling half her glass with whisky.

He pretended to look for it below the table and then admitted sheepishly, "I think it is over."

"You know I can't have my drink without it; just arrange it," she snapped.

Victoria and Azaad Nagar (V-AN)

Victoria and Azaad Nagar (V-AN) were sister cities—two sisters as different as chalk and cheese. One spoke less and ate lesser, and the other had verbal diarrhoea and insatiable hunger. One projected understated elegance and the other in-your-face vulgarity. One learnt the art of living and the other learnt the art of survival. One was an aristocrat and the other a commoner. Azaad Nagar gained independence in 1947, whereas Victoria was always independent.

The twin cities were collectively known as V-AN with its own government. Over the years, the two siblings had come to coexist in an uneasy equilibrium. Victoria had become slightly more accessible to the people of Azaad Nagar and Azaad Nagar had become somewhat tolerable to the people of Victoria. There were also some perfunctory changes, like the new names of some roads and buildings. But by and large, both the cities had retained their character.

Large houses with even bigger lawns, golf courses, parks, luxury hotels, and designer shops, but most of all, an abundance of snobbery – Victorians lived in their own world.

Ramshackle houses, congested streets, squatters, beggars, heaps of dirt, but most of all, an abundance of misery—Azaad Nagar*ites* survived in their own world.

It was not that the Victorians did not welcome outsiders. They welcomed neo-rich, tech moguls and foreign-educated, but there was a threshold; a certain escape velocity was required for an electron to jump from the orbit of Azaad Nagar to the orbit of Victoria and only a few were able to achieve the feat.

Then there were a few who were in the outermost orbit of Azaad Nagar, just waiting for that last push to migrate, and many of them lived in *Dhobhi* Colony. Though it was abutting the posh Victoria, Dhobhi Colony was technically part of Azaad Nagar. The desire of the bourgeois to live near the rich and powerful drove the demand for houses in the colony high. When the original inhabitants of Dhobhi Colony, most of whom were washer men or drivers or security guards to the *Sahebs* of Victoria, got a whiff of that demand, they immediately went about exploiting it. They handed over their shanties to builders, who erected three-storied grotesque structures in its place—Builder Floors.

The cost-cutting was done by using cheaper building material and erecting wafer-thin walls so that even a feeble fart on one floor could be heard on the other. However, neither the landlords complained because it was far superior to their original habitat, nor did the buyers, because of the compelling prices.

Normally, the landlords kept one floor, and one went to the builder as compensation. The remaining were either sold or rented out. The original landowners preferred to keep the ground floor, as it gave them an option of opening a shop and put an end to their slavery and of their future generations. Most opened grocery stores. Still, more adventurous types started garages, mobile phone shops and even unisex full body spas.

Ashok Mehra's landlord took the safest route and ran a *paan* shop—an evergreen and safe business. Ashok hated they lived above a paan shop frequented by drunks till late night who got into brawls at the drop of a hat and passed lewd remarks and made obscene gestures at passers-by, including Mrs Mehra. But then, this was the price to be paid to live close to Victoria, and the

Mehras realised that as long as they didn't tell anyone their address, leave alone invite anyone to their house, it was alright. Despite its nuisance, the shop had its uses.

They never ran out of cigarettes and sodas.

Earthquake

"*Oye* Lovely, send six sodas," Ashok leaned on the balcony railing and shouted.

For a moment, she was tempted to push him and release all her pent-up anger in one stroke. Her prankish mind was picturing his fall—towel flying off mid-air and him crash-landing on his dick. She broke into a sudden fit of laughter as a confused Ashok looked at her.

"Will you clear the previous bill?" Lovely shouted back.

"Will do it tomorrow. Just get six sodas ... please." Ashok looked at him pleadingly.

He turned to look at her and muttered, "This fucker has started showing attitude."

"Screw him, just tell him to hurry," she replied, lost in thought.

The delivery was completed in the next ten minutes, and half an hour later, they were bordering on drunkenness.

"So, what exactly do you have in mind?" The liquor had relaxed him a little; though, given an option, he still preferred the warmth of his blanket.

She took a large swig, lit a cigarette, and looked up at the smog-filled sky. "God, only if I could have seen her wicked mind behind that façade," she sighed.

He wanted to say the same thing to her. *If only he could have seen hers before marrying her,* though she never cared much about the façade—she was the same inside out. He kept quiet, his fingers nervously rubbing the rim of the whisky glass, waiting in anticipation for what she was going to come up with.

After a brief period of silence, she said, "Do you know why I got manipulated?" When Ashok gave her a dumb look, she continued, "Because I wanted her acceptance, period... nothing else, neither money nor favours, just a normal mutual respect between two humans."

He knew she had wanted much more than that, but kept quiet.

"It's past midnight, and the deadline is over. We are officially at war now," she declared like a General addressing the troops.

"But you are assuming the worst; like I said, things may change tomorrow. I think you are jumping the gun; remember that you have known each other for long."

She immediately replied with a smirk, "You know, there is one difference between people like you and people like me. Your kind close their eyes when they see a train coming right at them, hoping and praying it will somehow stop on its own. People like me act. We reverse the rotation of the wheels so that it breaks our enemies into pieces. You are a pigeon. I am a hawk."

Wounded to be called a pigeon, he retorted, "So, what exactly do you plan to do? How are you going to change the rotation of the wheels?" He didn't hide the sarcasm.

"That is something I need to figure out and which I will and there's another thing."

"What?"

"An hour back. She removed me from M&S."

This time, he felt a genuine hurt in her voice. He knew that, amongst all things, the M&S was most important to her; it was all that she lived for.

"That's terrible," he said, and tentatively placed his palm on her shoulder to console her.

She shrugged him off. "Don't worry, I will make her life hell. It's not important how you start a war; what's important is how you end it."

It was difficult to beat her in the game of wits. He could see that beneath passion and bravado on display, she was thinking hard and with every passing moment, her facial features were changing. There was a familiar mischievous glint in her eyes and her face had turned grisly, reminding him of movie gangsters who, after finalising their sinister plan, revisit each step-in mind, marvelling at their cunningness and celebrating their future triumph.

She suddenly put her feet on the table and took deep drags from her cigarette. As her overcoat rode up, he looked at her bare legs, long and slim. He knew she was deliberately exposing herself to seduce him. He was still under her spell when, in a sudden movement, she extended her arm and untied the knot of his towel.

As if on cue, the tectonic plates shifted somewhere in the Himalayas and an earthquake measuring 7.1 on the Richter scale shook their house. "*Bhukump aa gaya,*" she guffawed as she climbed on him.

Lightning and rain followed as she started moving rhythmically on top of him, touching his pleasure points to turn him on. She was in the middle of her act when, suddenly; she felt a pair of eyes watching her. She looked up at the terrace ledge, and even though it was dark, she could identify him. The moment their eyes met, she let out an orgasmic cry and removed her jacket. In the following minutes, she kept tantalising the intruder on her terrace while working on her husband. Both finished simultaneously; one limped back to the bedroom, and the other staggered down the stairs. She continued drinking long after the act.

The intensity of the rain was increasing every second, but despite the cacophony of rain, wind, and lightning, Tanvi Mehra could only hear the song playing on the radio in the *paan* shop.

... Nayak nahi Khalnayak hun main... and all of a sudden, her path became clear to her.

She would be the villain in this story.

After polishing off the entire bottle, she went inside the house, took the SIM out of her broken phone, and inserted it in Ashok's.

A minute later, she sent out a message

"I will trigger an earthquake that will bury you forever."

The message was blue-ticked instantly.

Chintan Shivir

Venue: GKP HQ, Leafy Lane, Victoria

As soon as the cavalcade arrived at the final crossing, Leafy Lane reverberated with the chants of "Sidheshwar Bhaiya *Ji ki jai... ki jai... ki jai...*" He strained his eyes to peep at the crowd through the tinted windows of his SUV and instantly felt better.

Maybe things were not all that bad.

An enormous crowd was lined up on both sides of the street, fluttering the Garib Kalyan Party (GKP) flags. Though he knew that most of the cheerers were hired for a fixed sum of money with added incentives for those who delivered the party slogans in a shrill, high-pitched voice and/or who could climb trees and tie up the party flag on the branches, it still felt good. Since the courts had banned sticking posters on man-made walls, tree trunks and branches had come to be accepted as an eco-friendly option.

Flanked by two pilot motorcycles, the SUV trudged forward and encountered a crowd spilling onto the street at about fifty meters from headquarters. It was then he got a closer look at their drooping mouths and downcast eyes, and the reality struck him. It was not all that rosy as it had seemed from a distance. Beneath the optics, he could clearly see the anger and disappointment on those faces. Mouths lie, but eyes don't, though even the *ki jai* chants lacked the usual melodious enthusiasm.

"Is this the end?" he sighed and stepped out of the white SUV amongst clapping and cheering of his party workers.

He had just taken a few steps towards the *Durbar* Hall—the venue of *Chintan Shivir* when an unknown person rushed towards him and emptied a bucket of rose petals on his head. Unfortunately, the petals were wet and clung to his face and clothes. Most of the cabinet members standing on the porch to welcome the CM kept a straight face, but he could see a few were openly laughing. Without speaking or displaying any emotion, he extended his hand towards his personal secretary, Bhola Singh, who quickly produced a white hand towel for his boss. Sidheshwar Gupta tried wiping his face and kurta but gave up when he noticed that the wet petals were leaking colour. Later, a hunt was conducted to catch the culprit. It was discovered that the offender was hired by a local flower contractor who, since the incident, had gone missing after leaving a note seeking mercy for his innocent action, "I wanted to excel at my job."

The CM swore silently and then gave a disapproving look, first to Bhola standing behind him and then to Deputy CM Banke Singh standing beside him. Bhola made a helpless face and bent down, pretending to tie his shoelaces, but Banke was not going to cow down. "It's part of the tradition," he articulated and gestured to the CM to move ahead.

Same village, same education, same IQ, and same father—what separated Bhola and Banke were spunks, the reason one was a PA and the other Deputy CM.

The leaking rose petals were not the only reason for Sidheshwar Gupta's displeasure. He was facing far bigger problems. His party was on a ventilator, and the emergency contemplation camp was not a celebration of some kind but a last-minute CPR to somehow save his government, which was predicted to lose the forthcoming elections by a landslide.

He also hated to be referred to as *Bhaiya*. At fifty-five, neither he was a youth icon and, in that sense, brother to all, nor his ancestors were from the region where every gangster's name had *Bhaiya* suffixed permanently. He was an average-looking, bespectacled man, the son of a school principal and could have become a doctor, lawyer, or taken up any profession the middle-class dreams of, had *Guruji* not taken him under his wings and ensured his entry and success in politics.

What a success it was!

Five years back, he had surprised the political pundits and bookies alike when his newly formed Garib Kalyan Party had trounced a longstanding government. It was a classic David v/s Goliath contest, but when the tide started turning, everyone rooted for the underdog, especially the people of Azaad Nagar, and made Sidheshwar Gupta the chief minister of Victoria-Azaad Nagar (V-AN).

His first six months in power were smooth. After receiving a landslide mandate, he had started off in earnest and had passed a series of laws to fulfil his electoral promises. He had even reached out to his opponents, seeking their cooperation to transform V-AN into a global city. However, he soon realised that implementation was not as easy as making promises. The unyielding bureaucracy, political compulsions, attacks by his opponents and even his own party men made him take two steps back for each step forward. Thereafter, the remaining term was a rough ride with him living from crisis to crisis; now, as he was about to complete his term, the very same issues—onion prices, corruption, inflation and law and order—which he had taken up aggressively to dethrone his opponent had come back to haunt him.

Guruji was smart. As soon as he had sensed that his protégé's popularity was declining, he had gone into hibernation. Unfortunately for him, Guruji had surfaced six months back and had issued veiled statements against him and his government, to the delight of his opponents.

Initially, he had not reacted, but since the first set of opinion polls hit the channels a couple of months back, he was desperately trying to reach out to his ex-mentor. He had even sent an invitation to Guruji to attend the *Chintan Shivir* as a *Margdarshak* (guide): "Guruji, I need you more than ever," he had enclosed a handwritten request with a box of *ladoos,* which Bhola had carried all the way to Guruji's village. Neither the invitation nor the ladoos were accepted.

To make matters worse, a week after Bhola's visit, Guruji declared to the media that he would undertake fast until death at Victoria Park against the ruling government until his demands were met. Having seen it first-hand, Sidheshwar was well aware of the power of Guruji's fast. He had been the beneficiary when Guruji had shut his mouth five years back. Now, it was payback time.

Even though he was red-faced in a red kurta, he forced a smile for the sake of the cameras. His cabinet followed him, and together they entered the Durbar Hall. A few seconds later, the entire cabinet retraced their paths because of the nauseating smell of the room freshener, which had been sprayed rather liberally. A furious Banke caught the collar of the housekeeper, who pleaded mercy and requested everyone, including the CM, to stand outside for a few minutes, during which he would ventilate the room.

The entire cabinet stepped out except for Meenakshi Tandon, who kept working on her laptop in the far corner of the hall. Sidheshwar caught sight of her and instructed Bhola to bring her over. Bhola covered his nostrils with a handkerchief and walked towards Meenakshi.

"You seem to be immune to the smell," Sidheshwar asked as soon as Meenakshi joined him.

"Not actually; I have been advising the poor fellow to go slow on the freshener, but guess he ignored me because he wanted to impress you," she replied, looking amusedly at his red-stained kurta.

He followed the movement of her eyes and said, "So, were you not outside when flowers were showered on me?"

"Oh … I missed the fun." Meenakshi arched her left eyebrow and giggled. Siddheshwar joined her, and just for a few moments, all his tensions evaporated.

She made him feel light and easy; she always did.

The two used to be neighbours and classmates. As the years passed, the rivalry in academics and sports gave way to a liking. It was more than that, and they would have consummated their relationship if she had not flown abroad seeking greener pastures. He was heartbroken. To forget her, he immersed himself in politics and eventually married someone else. As time passed, her memories kept fading, but not completely.

Midway through his term, he had asked her to join his cabinet. She agreed and left her prestigious lectureship abroad to become the Information and Broadcasting Minister. He sought her out not only to rekindle their connection but also because of her impressive credentials.

"How bad is it?"

"Very," she replied matter-of-factly and added, "If another term doesn't work out, you can join me in the States. I can get you a job, or we can start a business." She winked.

He looked at her and resisted the powerful urge to embrace her.

"I will keep that in mind," he said somewhat tersely and walked inside the Durbar Hall. His cabinet followed him, and within seconds, the contemplation camp begun with the repugnant smell still lingering in the air.

In addition to all the ministers, the camp was also attended by Bhoomi Pracharak, the chief editor and owner of the AAM Channel. He was a well-known supporter of the GKP and a trusted adviser to the CM. He was there to give insights into the public mood and media perception. During the prime time debate, he would harass all the detractors of GKP with his acerbic wit.

As soon as everyone sat down, Banke Singh got up from his chair. As number two in the government, he believed that it was his right to set the tone and agenda of the meeting, so he wanted to be the first speaker. He moved his chair, and with an effort, raised his burly frame. There was a time when he was a professional wrestler, swift and agile, but had gained much weight over the years, which his knees struggled to support. He was about to open his mouth when Siddheshwar dismissed him with a wave of the hand and then looked towards Meenakshi, whose head was still buried in the laptop.

"Meenakshi, I first want you to give us an overview of where we stand."

Banke turned red, and his lips started quivering. "Let's first sing our party song before this computer lady takes over," he said in a voice laced with anger and mirth.

CM looked at him calmly and said with an impassive face, "Banke Ji, I have had enough of this *tamasha* now. Please calm down and listen; you will be the first to speak after she finishes."

Banke was tempted to bite back, but kept quiet and sat back on his chair with the look of a sullen child.

"Meenakshi, please commence."

Meenakshi pressed a button to project her laptop onto the video wall and a series of histograms appeared on the screen. "The charts that you can see depict the cumulative results of opinion polls to date or what they call poll of polls. As you can see, our best-case scenario is twenty-two per cent of the votes, which in the worst case can go down to less than ten per cent."

Siddheshwar felt the earth shifting beneath his feet. He was aware of the desperate situation, but for an incumbent party to get less than ten per cent would be the first time in the electoral history of the state.

"Meenakshi, this is absurd. How can we go so low? After all, I have fulfilled all of my promises—the citizens have been enjoying free electricity and water under my rule for the last five years…this is impossible," he said in disbelief.

Banke took this as a cue and slammed his fists on the table. "I told you these computer people know nothing about politics; ask me, I have seen it all, and what is this ten per cent? Even if people from only my region vote for us, we will cross twenty-five per cent."

"You are right, but they will not vote for us, and the reason is you. You have again come up as the worst performing minister for the fifth year in a row," Meenakshi hit back.

Banke looked at CM and said accusingly, "Is this what I get in return for serving you faithfully for so many years? Someone who has not fought an election in her life is now publishing my report card."

"Banke ji…please stay calm; neither the party nor I have forgotten your contribution. Please let her finish," Sidheshwar said evenly.

Meenakshi pointed the laser at the declining curve and continued, "The government's popularity has been steadily declining over the past year, but an inflexion point came around 15 October. If the elections were held before that date, I would say that we had a fair chance, but not anymore."

"Why…what happened on 15th?" Siddheshwar looked at Bhola, who sheepishly shrugged.

"I guess it was an unremarkable day as any," the CM quipped.

"Something happened that day, but I will let Bhoomi take on from here."

Bhoomi asked for the next slide, which had just one line written in bold letters:

Victoria-Azaad Nagar has ranked lowest on the Happiness Index

"What is this?" A puzzled Sidheshwar asked.

"These are yearly rankings taken out by a prominent magazine. They undertake a survey which they call 'Mood of the Nation'. Nobody reads these surveys, but this time, there was a concentrated campaign by the opposition. Numerous opposition rallies were held to highlight this index, and it was also broadcasted on WhatsApp of every citizen."

"Happiness ... are you serious? Isn't it something internal? I have been CM for the last five years, and I am the most unhappy. Free electricity, free water, and even free rations ... Is their greed bottomless? Should I now do stand-up comedy to make them happy?"

There was silence in the room before Banke butted in, "*Saale ahsaan faramosh* (thankless people). If we keep giving in, they will milk dry the boobs of the state."

"Sid, these are the findings of our study. Now we are here to discuss and see if these are credible pointers," Meenakshi said coolly.

Banke glared at Meenakshi. How dare she take the first name of CM, that too in short form? Meenakshi ignored him and looked towards Bhoomi for support.

"In the end, it's your call, but as a media person, I must tell you that somehow people are unhappy, and you will have to do something soon to make them happy," Bhoomi said, rubbing his glasses.

Everyone in the room was pretending to contemplate when suddenly the lights went off, and the screen died.

There was confusion for a few seconds before Banke thundered at the caretaker, "How can they cut electricity in *Durbar Hall* when an important meeting is in progress?"

Having taken the flak for the room freshener fiasco, the caretaker was in no mood to accept further responsibility. "Electricity is not my responsibility," he replied in a raised voice.

"What do you mean by that, you pissant?" Banke shot back.

"Saheb, please don't insult my caste or else I will complain about the commission for the downtrodden."

Banke was taken aback. The downtrodden commission had a formidable clout, especially around elections. To firefight, he quickly changed his demeanour and smiled apologetically. Then he looked at the GKP treasurer and asked, "Didn't we pay the bill?"

Sidheshwar didn't wait for the treasurer's response. "Isn't electricity free for all?"

"It is free, but it is not available. The last stock of coal ran out last night. It's in the papers," the caretaker grimaced.

"Let's shift to Diplomat. They have backup," someone suggested.

One Two Cha Cha Cha

One two cha cha cha. Let's do cha cha cha.

She was moving back and forth, synching the jerks of her waist and taps of her feet to the beats. The sweat made her face shine and her clothes cling, but her gyrations were having no effect on her client, who just stood there, barely acknowledging her efforts with a soft grin.

The personal fitness training for Kiku Kapoor, the chairman of Gulab Chand Industries (GCI), was being held at the terrace of Kapoor villa—a 1000 sq. yard bungalow located at the exact geometric centre of Victoria.

The trainer was his wife's idea. "You need to get in some shape. It is a make-or-break time for you," she had reasoned, but Kiku was not ready to listen to any of it. To him, exercising meant moving one's body for no real purpose, something that he considered sacrilege. Despite numerous efforts by his father, Gulab Chand Kapoor, the founder of GCI and an avid sportsman, Kiku never took to a sport and eventually became obese at a young age.

It was only after his personal secretary showed him Malaika's Insta feed that Kiku relented. It was not her fit and tan body that caused the change of heart, but the compassion he saw in her eyes. Above everything else, Kiku was a succour for kindness, the one thing he felt that the world had deprived him of. Not only did he agree to the training, but in anticipation, stocked up on expensive fitness wear and 'zero gravity' shoes.

This was their third session together. In their first two sessions, he could barely keep up with her after the first ten minutes. But today, he felt exhausted within the first few seconds. It was partly due to liquor-induced dehydration—his head ached, and his lips were parched, and partly in anticipation of the crucial meeting he was to attend in the next couple of hours. But then, looking at her slithering to the music in her tight sweatpants, he feigned enthusiasm and moved his bulky posterior but gave up after a few steps.

"Sorry, my mind is somewhere else today," he apologised.

"No problem, Sir, you are doing very well. Let's do some stretching now, and we will be done for the day." She forced a smile of appreciation.

He loved stretching. After their first class, she had taken his hands into hers and had forcefully twisted his body in unimaginable angles, making him aware of the bones and muscles in his body, wrapped inside multiple layers of fat. It was painful, yet sweet, an erotic pain of a kind he had never experienced before.

Today, she proceeded with soft stretches, moving his arms from side to side, making him ache. He wanted the one in which she lifted him on her back.

"*Woh back wali,*" he said shyly.

She reluctantly turned around, and they stood with their backs touching each other as she entangled his arms with hers. She took a deep breath while praying for her well-being and then lifted his large body from the ground. It had seemed impossible the first time, but once she did it, she realised it was not too difficult. He was mainly made of alcohol and water.

After a couple of seconds, he started doing *aah* and *ouch.*

"*Bas, bas,*" he finally cried in pain.

She held him for some more time, deriving sadistic pleasure while he agonised and ranted. At last, she released him, and he landed on the ground with a thud.

"Thank you so much," he managed to mumble, still red-faced and panting.

As if on cue, a servant appeared with the tray, carrying coconut water for them.

He took a sip and wiped the sweat from his brow. "Sorry, Malaika, my mind was elsewhere. I am meeting some investors."

"All the best, Sir. I think you are fully prepared after this workout." She faked enthusiasm.

"Thank you. Thank you. Tomorrow, I will be more vigorous. You know, one-two." He comically moved in slow motion. "We also need to plan a massage session at least once a week. Stretching and massaging works best for me."

She was repulsed at the thought of giving a massage to a hippo, but then, he was a wealthy client, the wealthiest she had ever had, the one who could open many doors for her, and the one who could help her launch her dream—her own studio.

"Sure, Sir, from next week."

"Good, good." Kiku was mighty pleased.

"OK, Sir, I will take your leave now. And all the best once again for your meeting."

"Wait, I have got something for you," he said and picked the gift-wrapped box from the table and handed it to her.

"Thank you so much, Sir," she said excitedly and gave him a hug.

Later, Kiku stood under the shower, imagining the upcoming massage session. He came out of the bathroom light hearted and happy. It was a great start to an important day. He was midway through his *aloo paratha* when the news flash spoilt his mood.

GCI shares locked in at lower circuit at 14.80

Kiku let out a cry, "Is this the end?"

Hydrangeas

Half an hour's walk in the morning was her daily ritual. A half an hour to soak up the sun and tend to her collection of hydrangeas. Also, half an hour to plan her day and her future, which looked rather bleak.

She was walking in her tan-coloured Tod loafers and passing instructions to the two resident gardeners of Kapoor villa. The senior gardener was fiercely loyal to her mother-in-law, so he just half-listened and did not even bother to acknowledge. The junior, Rameshwaram, considered her a goddess and for a reason.

She had lifted him from the slums and placed him in a palace. None in the Kapoor clan knew that Rameshwaram was her distant cousin because there was no visible evidence to suggest that. She was extremely fair with deep blue eyes, and he was as black as black could be, though a discerning eye would pick similar unibrows.

Rameshwaram knew nothing about gardening, but that was not what he was hired for. She had wanted a pair of eyes and ears in Kapoor villa, and Rameshwaram didn't disappoint. A natural actor, he pretended not to understand English, Hindi or Punjabi—the language of choice in the Kapoor household.

He also kept his mouth shut at all times, a trait which gave him a virtual free pass to eavesdrop at will, as everyone considered him both deaf and dumb besides being an idiot. In reality, Rameshwaram was more educated than the Kapoor clan and read literary novels in his free time. He was watering the lawn, carefully avoiding the path she was tracing. Even then, a few drops did fall on her feet, sending a tingling sensation up her spine.

She was on the last leg of her walk when she saw her husband's personal trainer walking towards the gate. There was a spring in her step, which she guessed was because of the box in her hand. The latest iPhone was a *guru dakshina* from her student. She had seen the box in Kiku's study and had immediately guessed whom it was meant for.

Suddenly, she felt angry. Not because of the gift. Kiku habitually gave expensive gifts, hoping to earn loyalty and respect in return. Money could buy everything had been drilled into his nut at a very young age by his mother.

What made her angry or rather envious was the youthful exuberance on display. The way the trainer had roughly tied her hair in a bun, her tiny sports bra barely concealing her washboard abs and the tattoo at the nape of her neck, not to mention her lithe, athletic body.

She took out her phone and switched it to the selfie mode. After trying different angles, she felt disappointed. Despite being regarded as the most beautiful woman in the city, she knew that her looks were slowly withering away. Although she took good care of herself, the lines on her forehead were getting more pronounced, and her face looked a bit bloated.

Going under the knife was an option she had discarded long back, but she was having a rethink. She instantly resolved to spend more time in the gym and eat even less. She sucked in her cheeks and raised her eyebrows and involuntarily pressed the button.

"Hi, ma'am. Can I take a selfie with you?" Malaika was standing right in front of her.

For a moment, she was embarrassed to be seen clicking selfies like a teenager. After all, she was Soundarya Kapoor—the Czarina of Victoria. She was regularly featured in vanity magazines, which described her as an eternal beauty, a philanthropist, a caring wife, and a loving mother.

She swiftly brought her hand down and put the phone in the back pocket of her pyjamas.

"I was just trying out something. Not actually clicking selfies," she replied consciously.

"Can I have a picture with you, ma'am, please?" Malaika pleaded.

Soundarya gave a reluctant nod and signalled to Rameshwaram, who threw the water hose aside and came running towards her. Malaika passed her phone to him and showed him the button to press to take pictures. As Rameshwaram clicked, they stood in front of rows of pink, red, and yellow hydrangeas. For the last one, Malaika put her arm on Soundarya's shoulder. Soundarya initially flinched, but then kind of liked the smell of salty sweat and let her.

"You should have used your new phone," Soundarya said with a knowing smile. Even though she tried, she could not hide the envy and suspicion in her eyes, which made Malaika feel like a thief.

"Ma'am, all of a sudden Sir gave this to me, I need to learn all its functions. I am so excited. By the way, Kiku Sir is making some excellent progress." Malaika desperately wanted to change the topic.

Soundarya responded with a plastic smile, because she knew it was a white lie. Kiku hated moving his body as much as he hated hard work.

"That's good. I hope all your efforts pay off. He desperately needs to shed some weight."

"Ma'am, just give me six months, and you will see a brand-new Mr Kapoor."

Soundarya wanted to tell her that they didn't have six months but kept quiet. She knew it was Kiku's lust that was making him dance to her tunes, but then she was the one who had suggested a personal trainer in the first place. Even then, she didn't mind her husband's infatuation with a girl the same age as his daughter.

All said and done, Kiku was a good husband, and deep within, she too loved him, not in a romantic way, which was never the case, but more like parental love. Kiku depended on her for everything, virtually letting her make all the decisions at home and in business. Both the kids were abroad, pursuing their dreams, which meant burning money at an alarming rate.

There were no six months.

Things were turning bad to worse pretty fast. It had all started around two months back after a brokerage house ostensibly called Bear Investment came up with the report on GCI, containing allegations that the company was cooking books over the years and the company's net worth was negative.

The GCI stock plummeted by 20 per cent on the day the report was published. The auditors resigned, and the consequent delay in publishing the quarterly results kept the rumour mills turning, resulting in stock price dropping a further 50 per cent. Even after the results were finally published, the stock took a further beating, and though the price over the last fortnight was steadying but with a downward bias.

The GCI problems were not new to insiders. If not for some creative bookkeeping, the company would have folded a couple of years ago. But then after that sensational report by Bear, the auditors had finally raised their hands when they realised that signing off on the balance sheet could put all of them in jail. A bolder audit firm was appointed as a replacement, but the damage had already been done.

She tried to block the worrying thoughts and looked at Malaika, who was now clicking the pictures of the bungalow.

"This is private property. Please don't post this on social media. Same goes for our pics together," she said petulantly.

"Sure, ma'am, I was anyway not going to do it," Malaika replied nervously. She was taken aback by the sudden change in Soundarya's mood.

"Also, can you cover your body with a jacket or shawl when you come and leave the house? There are many male servants in this house."

Malaika felt naked. She tried to pull her bra down to cover her waist, but the Lycra didn't budge a centimetre.

"You say my husband is making progress; that's good, but I would like to see some quantifiable progress in terms of kilos lost," she said like a warning.

"Sure, ma'am, but I have to go slow with him because of his medical history."

"What medical history? So now, you are also a doctor. I don't want any excuses. I am paying you top dollar and my husband is showering you with gifts. In return, keep your end of the bargain; trainers like you are a dime a dozen. Consider yourself fortunate that we selected you."

Malaika eyes welled up.

"Yes, ma'am," she mumbled and slowly started walking out.

Soundarya noticed her shoulders were drooping, and she was digging her feet into the ground, a far cry from the confident walk a while back. She had successfully killed her exuberance.

She slyly watched the girl till she got into an auto rickshaw. The moment she disappeared from her sight; her heart filled with pity for the girl. As tears rolled down her cheeks, she cursed herself for humiliating a girl the same age as her daughter and that too for no reason other than her own insecurities. She knew her outburst was involuntary, a side effect of anxiety and worry that were not letting her sleep at night. She let the remorse ooze out before entering the bungalow.

Later, she sat smoking on the veranda adjoining her bedroom on the first floor. She was glad that no one had protested Tanvi's removal from the group. This was a minor victory in what was going to be a long war. For now, her boat was steady, but currents could change without warning.

Tanvi Mehra was a formidable enemy, a venomous snake, a fighter who doggedly pursued her goals, and she would not leave any stone unturned to take her revenge. She had read her threatening message several times before deleting it and blocking her. The rising tension made her open the market tracker, and the moment she found the GCI stock was locked in the lower circuit, her hand trembled, and she let out a sigh. "Is this the end?"

Dhobhi

Over twelve hours had passed since Tanvi Mehra was removed from M&S, despite that, she didn't get a single message from anyone. Her adversary, Soundarya Kapoor, had money, and money bought everything—friendship, loyalty and power. Still, she had expected some to side with her or at least fake sympathy.

She had curry favoured many, but none, not even one, had reached out. But then, wasn't it expected? Didn't she know the deal? They were not friends, only fair-weather acquaintances, and as soon as her boat rocked, the rats left.

She would swallow the poison now, but would eventually make them repent. She may not be as rich and influential, but her cunningness and resourcefulness could even make Machiavellianism pale in comparison.

The rains had not stopped since last night, and the flooding on the roads was all over the news. The TV was live streaming CM Siddheshwar Gupta sailing on a dinghy, carrying relief material for the homeless.

"Asshole," she swore and lit a cigarette. After a couple of satisfying drags, she noticed the broken flowerpot and the memories of last night started seeping into her mind. She had no idea how it broke, whether it was the thunderstorm or the victim of her drunken fury. It was all hazy, though she remembered her other victims, especially the one who was watching her from the terrace.

It was evil of her to manipulate the malleable mind of a boy who probably had just hit puberty and expose it to such levels of ecstasy.

She remembered the bewilderment and agony on his face. It was as if he had seen a ghost, but everything had happened in the spur of the moment, a moment in which she felt like a predator. She laughed, clasped her hands and looked at the sky to atone for her sins.

She finished her coffee and went inside the living room, where Ashok was pacing up and down in his worn-out elastic shorts, pleading with someone on the phone. She guessed it was a loan shark that he was talking to. It was his only hope to get a loan as the maxed-out cards had plunged his credit rating so much that banks had declared him persona non grata.

She remembered the EMI reminder. It was for her car loan repayment. In anticipation of its confiscation by the bank, she had already started parking it at her friend's place. "My garage is already packed with three cars," she had lied.

Her husband finished the call and cried in dejection, "He said no."

Ashok Mehra's business had been in the doldrums ever since the government had implemented the free Electricity and Water Scheme, but he blamed his wife for everything. He had been a successful *dhobhi,* happily running a profitable laundry until she made him sell it to start a solar business he knew nothing about.

His college degree was fake, but his wife kept pestering him to get into a respectable business. She was part of the elite circle, and keeping up appearances was vital for her. He eventually gave in and sold the profitable laundry for an apparently reputable business that never took off.

Free electricity by Siddheshwar Gupta was one of the reasons; his lack of effort was another.

Once GKP brought free electricity, no one was interested in saving on the bill. Only a few wealthy in Victoria spent on installing solar panels in their homes, either as atonement for burning fossil fuels in their monster SUVs/jet planes or to establish their credential as an environmental crusader—an in-vogue fashionable avocation.

So, that way, the market had shrunk considerably, but then, Ashok was also a taciturn man who preferred sitting at home to getting out there. He had given up long ago and was left with piles of debt and a high-maintenance wife.

"What do you want me to do?" She asked him.

"Sell your car," he replied immediately.

"That's your plan to make me let go of one decent thing I have," she replied furiously.

The fifty lakh plus luxury sedan was Tanvi's passport to social life. Despite her being well spoken, witty, and a looker, the gentry of Victoria only allowed those in their inner circle who were above a certain minimum threshold in terms of personal wealth, and the car enabled her to keep up false appearances.

"I don't see any other way. If you sell your car, we can survive for a couple of months, and hopefully, I will be able to restart the laundry by then," Ashok reasoned.

"You fuckin *dhobhi*. No way am I allowing you to start laundry, and no way would I sell the car," she snarled.

"I have tried everything possible. No one wants this solar stuff," he said helplessly.

"You lazy fuck, try harder. Go out there, meet people, talk to them, influence them, and make bonds."

"Why don't you make bonds? As such, you are on every man's wish list," he shot back.

Tanvi swiftly moved her right hand to pick up the empty whisky bottle from the kitchen counter. She nearly missed the bullseye.

Ashok was rushed to the hospital, where he was administered ten stitches half an inch above his right eyebrow.

M&S

Human beings yearn for exclusivity because they want to feel unique and special. They pay through their nose to travel first class. They dream of living in upscale neighbourhoods. They prefer bespoke experiences. They seek privacy and the illusion of increased worth, but most importantly, they strive to set themselves apart from the crowd. Movers and Shakers (M&S) was founded by Tanvi Mehra and Soundarya Kapoor to exploit this hunger.

Tanvi was the one who had come up with the idea a couple of years back.

"Why don't we launch a social club?"

"What will that club do?" Soundarya had replied absentmindedly.

"It will be a private members club. We will admit whoever we want."

"But what will it do?"

"Parties, holidays and even charity; pretty much everything rich do."

"Why take the headache of managing all that crap?"

"For kicks. There's nothing to invest in. We just have to create a WhatsApp group and add people who make the cut. It would be an eclectic mix of people who are wealthy, powerful, and even talented. We can even include a few arty types. If we do it well, soon, entry into our group will be more sought-after than Gymkhana."

Soundarya had brooded for a while before putting a condescending hand on Tanvi's shoulders. "But then, we can only have people from Victoria. How will you be a part of all this?"

Tanvi knew Soundarya was deliberately touching her raw nerve. That was the reality of their friendship. Soundarya never missed an opportunity to convey that it was an act of benevolence on her part. Tanvi was torn but kept a straight face.

"You will be president, and I will be secretary, and in any case, Ashok's business has turned a corner, and soon, we will be on this side of the city," Tanvi lied.

M&S's first party was hosted at the lawns of the Diplomat. It was attended by A-listers, including politicians, industrialists, diplomats, bureaucrats, stars and gangsters. The organisers left no stone unturned to make it a grand success, including serving the best champagne, caviar and even belly dancers. The party got extensive coverage on page three, and in no time, everyone wanted to be a part of M&S.

Under Soundarya's stewardship, Tanvi Mehra ran the group with an iron fist. She had control over who would throw a party and where. The food and wine list had to be concurred by both Tanvi and Soundarya. When a member challenged their authority, they would be expelled without notice.

Also, the founders would use their formidable influence to ensure that the traitor was not invited to any social event or party in the city and was rendered a social outcast. Many begged and cried to be readmitted. A few got admitted back, but with a strict warning that they must be forever pliant.

M&S partied at least once a week. However, since the fallout of the founders, there was no information on the next party. This made the members restless, but no one could propose a party without the prior approval of admins. Another strong itch to meet up was to gossip about the showdown between Tanvi and Soundarya and gauge which way the wind was blowing. So, they met privately.

Toni-Moni and Dubeys meet at the Royal Salute.

As soon as Toni opened his mouth to ingest tiramisu pastry, Moni kicked her husband with the sharp edge of her Louboutins. Toni was a perennially hungry, carnal man who ate, drank and spent money as if there was no tomorrow. Today, once again, he had gone berserk. He had ordered a bottle of 18-year-old Macallan and crabs to go along with it. *Now, who does that at the insanely pricey Royal Salute?* Moni cursed in her mind.

The clever Dubeys had just sat through the evening, sipping the cheapest wine on the list and nibbling couscous salad. Moni hated crabs, salads, and whisky. She had ordered tandoori chicken and periodically gulped vodka shots, frowning at her uncouth husband. He was making a fool of himself.

His face and shirt were smudged with butter-garlic and shells, and his voice progressively slurred with each drink. Still clueless of his gross manners, he had dug deep and devoured the last vestiges of his second female crab of the evening. *Now, what was this crab business?* She rued.

They had both loved tandoori chicken earlier, but since he had started taking trips to Seychelles, crab was all he wanted. A female one too. She knew what was going to happen in the end. The Dubeys would sneak out, or, at the most, offer to contribute for their glasses of wine and *ghas phus,* leaving Toni to clear the bill. Asking them for dinner was a mistake, but she desperately wanted to gossip, and Dubeys were the only ones free.

"No message on the group since the bitch was thrown out," Moni said, looking at her phone.

"All are *fattus*. No one has the guts to take sides," Toni slurred.

"But I am happy. She deserved it," Moni countered.

"Why? What did she do to be thrown out of the party and removed from the group? In fact, M&S is entirely Tanvi's show,

Soundarya Kapoor can't do shit without her. It was her good luck that I was not there at that party that night or else ...," Toni challenged.

"Bullshit, Tanvi is a nobody. I spoke to Shaina, who told me she lives in *Dhobhi* Colony." Moni smirked.

"So, what? Your forefathers also lived there. Do you think Soundarya was born in Victoria?" Toni thundered.

"Maybe not, but now she is the wife of the owner of GCI."

"*Behenchod*. Don't remind me of GCI. I lost a bundle on its shares."

"Arrey, how's that relevant? Soundarya is class, and Tanvi Mehra is a parasite who has been sponging off Soundarya, and finally, Soundarya saw her true colours; good riddance," Moni scoffed.

"I am with Tanvi, and I am calling her," Toni declared and took out his phone.

"If you do that, you will see my dead face," Moni warned.

Toni chuckled and signalled the server to refill his whisky.

"Are you insane? More *daaru* after food," Moni shouted.

Toni was unmoved by his wife's protest and asked the server to hurry.

Tarandeep (Toni) and Manpreet (Moni) ran a chain of banquets named 'Made in Heaven', but actually, it was their pairing that was made in heaven; at least, until Toni ditched tandoori chicken for crabs. Both belonged to wealthy families and had identical IQs, plus or minus.

Dubeys sat there, listening to the mad couple, regretting why they had agreed to the dinner. KD Dubey, the former Income Tax Commissioner, was a living legend, not because he had served the state but because of the wealth he could amass rendering that service, including an eighty-crore bungalow in Victoria Lane. The years of service had taught him never to give an opinion in public or take a stand. He elbowed his wife, Suman Dubey, to leave, but she was busy eating the last bits of couscous.

He finally mustered courage and said, "Shall we call it a day?"

"Wait, which side are you on?" Toni asked KD threateningly.

"We are neutral," KD stuttered.

"That is because you are *fattu*; both of you."

"How can we intervene? The matter is between two co-founders," Suman Dubey said like a lawyer.

Toni looked at Moni and said, "These guys are so dull and spunkless."

Moni nodded. "KD, you guys need to take a stand like us. Toni is with Tanvi, and I am with Soundarya."

"If you don't, I will make sure you pick up today's cheque," Toni added.

Hearing that, Dubeys sprang up from their chairs and ran towards the exit. Toni and Moni followed them, but stopped midway and broke into a fit of laughter.

"Good fun fucking them," Moni said.

"Ya, this was fun. I need another drink."

Later, over more drinks. "Why do you support that two-bit Tanvi? What do you find in her? I know you have a thing for her," Moni grumbled to her drunk husband.

"I like her, and I am sure she will emerge victorious. Though the odds may seem stacked against her, she is a savage," Toni slurred.

"Do you love me?" An emotionally drained Moni asked.

"Love you, honey," Toni murmured before vomiting on the table.

Gin-Tonic

The group of ministers reached Diplomat to continue contemplation, but their foremost agenda was to fill their bellies, so they all got busy hogging lunch except for their chief minister. Siddheshwar was nursing a gin-tonic in a suite on the fourteenth floor, the official residence of Meenakshi Tandon.

She had refused the government bungalow and chosen Diplomat instead. It was a luxurious accommodation with a floor-to-ceiling bar, a separate dining area and a massive bedroom with an ensuite bathroom embellished with Italian fixtures. The tariff was obnoxious and was funded by media companies, which needed the blessings of the minister.

She had texted him on their way to Diplomat, *Gin-tonic, my place?*

It was tricky for him to sneak up to her suite in the presence of his colleagues, but he had thrown caution to the winds and taken the elevator. He desperately needed to take his mind off his imminent defeat, and the idea of drinking with her was irresistible.

"What would you like to have for lunch? I recommend the crispy salmon with mashed potatoes," she suggested.

"Whatever, I am OK even with the Indian stuff, some dal and roti," he said, taking out a miniature Tanqueray from the bar.

"As you wish, let me ask for some yellow dal and roti. *Naan* or tandoori?"

"Plain tandoori, no butter. Also, I have asked Bhola to drop my change of clothes at the reception."

"Why don't you lie on the bed and relax for some time?"

Siddheshwar hesitated at first, but he was actually tired, both physically and mentally. He got up from the sofa and walked to the adjoining bedroom. As he sat on the edge of the bed, she teased him, "Don't be so shy. We have shared a bed in the past."

He shyly laughed and took out his sandals. He then adjusted the pillow for lumbar support and sat on the bed. She also did likewise; soon, they were comfortably sipping their gins, their arms touching intermittently.

"How is it to live in a hotel?" He asked.

"Convenient. I tried normal houses, but it was a failed experiment."

"We have come a long way. It seems like yesterday when we were in school."

"I still remember you had hit that bully Rajesh with the cricket bat, and he had to be rushed to the hospital."

"In fact, that was the day everything changed for me. I realized my strength, and the rest is history."

"Politics is a tough game."

"It is, and I somehow have been surviving. I was lucky things worked out for me; otherwise, how could an average middle-class guy become chief minister? I was satisfied with what I had achieved until you showed me the projections. Losing is one thing, but crashing out like that is shameful. It's over for me."

There was a gentle knock on the door, which made Siddheshwar stiffen. Meenakshi opened the door and was greeted by the server carrying the lunch trolley and a hanger, holding a neatly pressed shirt and trousers.

"Lunch is served, and your clothes are here."

Siddheshwar ambled to the dining table, made a roll of the tandoori roti, and took a large bite. He then looked at Meenakshi and said, "I don't want to lose. Tell me what the way out is."

Meenakshi took a cigarette from the case and lit it. "I smoke only one or two a day. What about you?"

"I quit the day I took the oath; cold turkey, but I would like a drag."

She passed the cigarette to him. He inhaled and coughed.

"Don't spoil your virgin lungs." She laughed.

He passed the cigarette back to her. She looked at him for a few seconds and then spoke thoughtfully, "One thing is sure, it is almost impossible for you to regain power until or unless something drastic is done in the next two weeks before the code of conduct kicks in. My projections and estimates, which made Banke bark, may be off a little, but it is sure that you are going to lose."

"You already told me this, and I have more trust in your analysis than that buffoon, Banke. I want to pick your thoughts on what can be done."

"I had a long discussion with Bhoomi. We agreed that you will have to do something which can have a disproportionate effect on the lives of the citizens. Something which your political rivals can't even imagine. Something bold, a game changer, something that can take the state to the top of the Happiness Index."

"What can that be?"

"There are a few ideas that we can work on. The problem is this contemplation camp will not work. People like Banke and others are too conservative to think of fresh ideas. We will have to exclude them."

"Done."

"Also, the first step you should take is to appoint someone as Happiness Minister. The people must realise that you are sensitive to their demands."

"Happiness Minister," Siddheshwar was thinking aloud.

"I know this sounds silly, but at least it will signal that you are serious about people's happiness."

Siddheshwar poured more gin for himself and her, and they spent a few quiet moments.

"Bhoomi also suggested that I should be that minister, ha-ha," Meenakshi said casually yet cautiously, using laughter as a camouflage.

This was the moment when everything could go right or wrong.

Though he kept an impassive face, Meenakshi could sense he was uncomfortable. He didn't like to be dictated by anyone. It was time to do damage control.

"Of course, he was not serious. Neither I am interested nor capable of taking on such a role. I would be happy to fly out if you lose and stay on as I&B if you win, provided you want me." She leaned on her American accent to impress that she didn't care.

As she said that, she noticed Siddheshwar's facial expressions loosening.

Show a man you don't care, and he will follow you like a puppy.

"What will this minister actually do?" He asked.

"My understanding is that such a minister would be the humane face of the government and instead of material stuff like *roti, kapda aur makaan,* would deal with the emotional state of citizens, their joy, satisfaction, contentment, fulfilment and all that spiritual bullshit. This will be a one-of-a-kind portfolio, never implemented even in the Western world. This will be your unique model of governance."

She had rehearsed these lines several times and wondered if they were convincing, except for the last line—the unique model of governance. Siddheshwar was proud of his unique model of free electricity and water. They spoke some more and later ordered coffee. Before leaving, Siddheshwar said, "Let's make it happen."

A wave of excitement swept through her body, but she didn't let it show on her face.

Investor Meet

Kiku would have made it on time had the heightened anxiety caused by the plunging GCI stock not triggered unexpected bowel movements. He had sat on the toilet seat, monitoring the gyrations of the stock price while desperately imploring god to make it rise. It rose, but every time it crossed 15, it was shorted mercilessly.

The short sellers were unknown to him, but he could imagine them huddled together in a room full of computers and relentlessly pressing the 'Sell' button. He could even spot a few bullies from his school. They were having a field day, destroying the 'tub of lard'. That was what his tormentors used to call him in school. Those were the most troubled years of his life and had left scars, which, even after decades, were fresh in his mind and soul.

He finally reached the business centre on the second floor of Diplomat, an hour late. All except Robert Brown got up from their chairs when he entered the conference room. Brown was the expat CEO of TWW and was well known in the business world for his ruthlessness. He gave Kiku a stern glare that turned his insides to jelly and then got busy with Candy Crush.

Robert was sitting at the head of the table, and a chair on his left was kept vacant for Kiku. At that moment, this insult bothered Kiku more than Brown's lack of courtesy. It was not as if Robert Brown was chairing the meeting. It was merely an exploratory meeting between GCI and TWW, which his wife had arranged. Each group was represented by lawyers and accountants; those belonging to

GCI were seated on the left of the table, and those belonging to TWW on the right.

"I am sorry for being late," Kiku mumbled shyly before somehow fitting into the chair. Brown didn't bother to acknowledge and kept crushing.

After a few embarrassing moments, Robert taunted, "I don't know how you do business, but where I come from, making one wait is either a sign of disrespect or a casual attitude."

Kiku could feel the palpitations in his heart. He was not good at confrontations. *Did he forget to take his medicine?* He turned back and signalled to his secretary, who rushed out of the conference hall.

Kiku was thinking hard to say something, something nice, something witty, and something to make the asshole stop embarrassing him in front of everyone. He had a powerful urge to drink and decided to stop by the Royal Salute after the meeting. He sheepishly scanned the room. The TWW team was beaming, and the GCI was despondent. Brown had won the match before even the first ball had been bowled.

Don't cow down. You are the chairman of GCI, he forcefully reminded himself, and tightly clenched his hands.

"*Atithi Devo Bhava,* you are like a god to us."

It was a well-thought-out beginning. After all, Brown was a foreigner and as such, foreign companies and goods were going out of favour. Everyone was vocal about the local. Brown raised his eyebrow but kept quiet.

"I am sorry for being late. I had an upset stomach and couldn't help it. I am a kind man, and if it was you, instead of me, who had come late due to reasons beyond your control, I wouldn't have made a mention of it to embarrass you. This is how I do business."

Kiku looked around the table and saw the look of admiration on his team. He continued, "Now, let's cut to the chase. I assume you have done the due diligence before you decided to meet, and now you are here, eager and early. Let's not waste time on frivolities and take this ahead with an open mind."

Brown was taken aback by the smoothness with which Kiku had delivered those lines. His research team had caricatured Kiku Kapoor as dull, egoistic and an anxious man, who quickly wilted under pressure. That was not entirely true. Kiku was smart enough to know that he wanted GCI. He changed his tactics. He extended his arm to shake hands with Kiku, but his firm grip made Kiku flinch. Both men were still testing each other.

"I am here with an open mind. Yours is a reputed brand. Still, its popularity is waning, and I am being polite here," Robert Brown said drily.

Pleased that Brown was taking him seriously, an encouraged and energised Kiku continued firmly, "To value a company like ours is not as straightforward. We have loyal customers who only trust us despite the glitz and glamour of newer brands. Our brand has inspired countless movie stars who have laughed, cried, romanced and fought under its influence. Our brand is known in every nook and corner of the country and is loved equally by the aristocrats and commoners. All this without spending a single paisa on marketing. My father, the founder of GCI, believed that marketing was akin to pimping. Our brand stands on its own legs."

Kiku hoped that his well-rehearsed lines would have the desired effect on Brown. He took a sip of water, wishing that it was whisky. Brown went silent, and it seemed like Deuce, Advantage—Kiku.

"The current price of your stock is 13.20."

Kiku's heart skipped a beat. *Wasn't 14.20 the lower circuit?*

"Mister Brown, you know markets don't follow logic."

"If you are so sure of that, why don't you buy back?" Brown retorted.

"We will. In fact, we will do it very soon." Kiku looked at his CFO, who anxiously nodded his head.

Brown chuckled. "I trust your intent, but I don't trust your capability. GCI is bankrupt, period; you know it, I know it, and all those people out there who are currently dumping your stocks, know it."

Kiku's heart again started beating so fast that he feared he would get an attack at any moment. He cursed his secretary. So much time to get a pill. He wanted to reason with Brown, but the words eluded him. He just wanted to get it over with.

"What's your offer price?" Kiku said, exasperated.

"Zero."

"What the fuck!" Kiku said and flung the papers in front of him.

"I will, however, take over all your debt. You will be a free man, unencumbered, with no burden, free to spend time with your lovely wife or, for that matter, drink all day at your favourite Royal Salute. Isn't that what you will do after this meeting?"

Kiku was bewildered. He had come to do the deal and had a figure in mind, but he could not believe the gall of the buyer who wanted his company for free. The rage rose in him and he hissed, "There is no point in discussing this further. You have wasted my time."

"Sleep over it. You have time till the weekend because after that, I will revoke my offer," Brown gave an ultimatum.

"You can shove your offer up your ass," Kiku shouted.

"Your call, you tub of lard," Robert Brown said and grinned.

As soon as the words were said, a 200 kg Kiku flew from his chair and landed on Brown's head, forcing him to fall out of his chair. The two entangled men rolled together on the floor, throwing indiscriminate punches at each other. Their respective teams struggled to separate them. It was difficult to determine who won, but both had blood. Later, Kiku entered the men's room and vigorously splashed water on his face to remove marks of blood and tears.

He took out his phone to call Soundarya, but his quivering fingertips dialled Malaika instead.

"Hello, Sir, how was the meeting?" She answered excitedly.

"Come to Royal Salute, I need you." He disconnected the phone without waiting for her to answer and broke down again.

Drop Out

Q1. Which was the largest city of Harappa civilisation? (1 mark) The question made him tremble with excitement. Still, he glanced through the remaining questions before conceding that Fattu was right. The question paper for which he had shelled out 50K was indeed the leaked one. He had had his doubts till that moment because Fattu was a gullible fool who could be coaxed into selling his kidneys for free.

Nevertheless, to be on the safe side, he had the answers on the cheat sheets tucked in his socks. What other option did he have? Memorising the answers was out of the question. He neither had the ability nor the interest. The reality was that he had long given up on education, and the only reason he was sitting for the exam was to qualify for a foreign visa.

He looked to his right and saw that Fattu was already looking towards him, displaying his large protruding teeth like a triumphant warrior. It was the most noticeable feature of his appearance, which covered almost half his face. That and sunken cheeks, which may have been desirable on a model, but were merely evidence of abject poverty and malnutrition on him.

His father was a municipality sweeper, barely earning enough to provide two meals a day to his family. He had a gaunt frame supported by matchstick legs. However, despite his visible physical inadequacies, Fattu was a daredevil who could punch anyone to death.

He was his best and only friend in the world.

Lovely met his gaze and muttered, *Behenchod,* and gestured him to look straight. There was no need to attract unnecessary attention till the job was completed. He looked at the invigilator sitting at the head table of the tiny classroom, digging into the plate of samosas. He was the school's PT teacher, a promising footballer many years ago whose dreams had ended when he had broken his leg, not on the football field but in a street brawl.

The job at school under the disability quota was an act of benevolence of the sports ministry. For years now, he was trying to drown his sorrows in alcohol and had grown a considerable paunch. Lovely was certain that he was drunk even at that moment and would snooze off after devouring the snack. He decided to make his move then. He wrote his roll number on the answer sheet and waited.

He closed his eyes and once again remembered last night. The scenes of midnight carnality that he had witnessed simply refused to vacate his mind. It was so overwhelming for him that he couldn't sleep all night despite masturbating thrice. Lying on the bed, he had shivered in turns with ecstasy and depression.

It was not as if he was a virgin. He and Fattu had visited the red-light area, but the experience was so stale, so colourless, so passionless that he had almost regretted doing it. Fattu had also admitted the same; though at first, he had lied about his exploits and how the prostitute had complimented him on his skills. But once the cat was out of the bag, they grudgingly convinced themselves that the extended orgies they saw in the blue films were under the influence of drugs.

They were wrong—Lovely couldn't wait to tell Fattu. It was last night that he had truly lost his virginity without even touching her body.

Even now, he just wanted to close his eyes and recreate the instant she had looked at him and taken off her jacket to give him a clear view of her body. Was it intentional? It surely was. Lovely smiled and hardened. He took out the compass from his geometry box and, using the needle of the pivot, started etching her name – TANVI – on the table.

He got so engrossed in his act that he lost track of time, and it was only when he heard the murmurs in the classroom that he looked up and noticed that the invigilator was snoring. He reluctantly kept the compass back in the box, determined that he would complete the job after writing the paper.

He took out the notes in a swift movement and placed them under the folds of the answer sheet. He took out the first sheet to find out the largest city of Harappa civilisation. He searched the sheet for the answer and was immediately confused, and after browsing the entire sheet, reality struck him. Instead of tucking in the answer sheets in his socks, he had mistakenly tucked in the paan shop ledger. The last entry on that ledger was:

Gandu – 6 soda

Gandu was his nickname for Ashok Mehra.

Lovely looked at Fattu, who was busy writing. He wanted to signal to him to finish fast and pass his papers to him. He just needed pass marks; anything above that was against his principles. As he waited for Fattu to look towards him, he heard a loud slap, followed by the choicest expletives—*Saale, nakal karta hai.*

Lovely snapped his face towards the sound and saw that the PT teacher was holding Kaalia by the collar and continuously slapping him. Kaalia was also a repeat student like him and Fattu and he had also laid hands on the leaked question paper. After a flurry of slaps, Kaalia started wailing loudly before leaving the room. Lovely just sat there, startled, too afraid now to even look at Fattu.

A few moments passed, and anger started clouding his mind. It was because of her he had mixed up the notes. She had fucked with his mind and had incapacitated him, and now all he wanted was her. He took out the compass from the geometry box and drew a picture of a vagina on the desk. He then drew a phallus entering that vagina.

After he finished, he got up from his seat, walked up to the invigilator, submitted the blank answer sheet and left. That was his last day at school. He was a dropout.

Breaking News

16 December

In a surprise move, Meenakshi Tandon has been sworn in as the Happiness Minister. The announcement that comes a fortnight before the model code of conduct kicks in has baffled political observers, opposition and even members of the ruling party.

The hush-hush oath-taking ceremony took place at midnight at the CM's residence. Soon after, Siddheshwar Gupta issued a brief statement:

"Tonight, we have made history by appointing the first-ever Happiness Minister of the state. It is the first time such a portfolio has been created anywhere in the world, and it is a testimony of GKP's unique governance model. The minister will work on war footing to bring happiness to our citizens."

Deputy CM Banke was absent at the swearing ceremony and has not spoken since.

The opposition has called this move laughable. "After extracting the last ounce of blood from citizens, they are now making fun of them. Anyway, it doesn't matter, this government is falling," said Solanki. His colleague, Bhure Prasad, was not so charitable and has called the new minister a foreign returned courtesan.

Bhoomi Pracharak, CEO and editor of the AAM channel, has said that it is a sensible move by the government as the state is lagging in the Happiness Index despite admirable governance by GKP in the last five years.

Meanwhile, social media is flooded with memes of Tandon performing hook steps to entertain the people.

Token

Soundarya asked the driver to drop her at the hotel's rear entrance, which only a few were aware of. The unknown caller had advised her to go unnoticed, which was almost impossible for her, particularly in her playground—Diplomat. Still, she wrapped her face in a scarf and wore oversized glasses. The plastic key to the suite on the fourteenth floor had been sent to her the night before.

As the glass elevator started ascending, Soundarya looked down at the expansive lobby. Even though it was familiar surroundings, she couldn't help but admire the opulence and the old-world charm. Persian rugs laid on Italian marble, chandeliers reminiscent of a philanderer Nawab's haveli, high ceilings, artwork, and bellhops in pristine uniforms.

The hotel had been built during colonial rule and depicted the lavish lifestyle of Rajas and Maharajahs. A pianist was playing the grand piano at the far end, filling the lobby with soothing jazz. The open-layout coffee shop and iconic Royal Salute bar were packed with guests indulging in gourmet cuisine and fine wines. She noticed familiar faces, acquaintances who spent their days in hotels. She saw a few eyes on her and looked away.

Till a few months back, the hotel was the second home to Kapoors. For years, a luxury suite was permanently booked for the family. However, once the GCI problems made headlines, the hotel revoked the lease, citing the accumulated dues of the past several years. That was not true, not entirely.

The hotel wouldn't have dared to do such a thing six months back. After all, Kapoors were the gold standard. The family was among the hotel's oldest patrons, and its famed library even had a portrait of Gulab Chand Kapoor. Even if they didn't pay up, the publicity of the city's oldest business family having a permanent suite was worth its weight in gold, but apparently no longer.

Soundarya tapped the key on the door sensor and was greeted by Meenakshi Tandon. The minister was in a casual tee and jeans and looked very different from how she appeared on TV in bright sarees and large *bindis. Bad camera angles make people look fat,* Soundarya thought, *and also the clothes.*

Up close, she saw a slim girl with delicate features, who had deliberately cultivated the rough, tough and hassled look to portray herself as a no-nonsense politician. They exchanged pleasantries and Meenakshi guided her to the living room.

Soundarya felt upbeat about the meeting until she saw him. Like many others in Victoria, she despised Bhoomi Pracharak, who had made it his mission to go after what he called the Victoria gang. The mission had made him very rich, and ironically, he now lived in a large bungalow in Victoria.

For Soundarya, it was a personal animosity. After the revelations by Bear Investment, Bhoomi Pracharak went after GCI with a vengeance and made *#houseofcards* go viral. Even worse, he had got personal, and for days, his AAM channel played video clips of M&S parties to create a perception that Kapoors, in addition to being crooks and incompetent, were also immoral.

She wanted to leave immediately, but her desperation stopped her. She needed to know why she was called.

"Congratulations, Meenakshi," she greeted Meenakshi and then gave a polite nod to Bhoomi.

"Thank you, Soundarya. Have you met Bhoomi before?"

"Not in person, I guess, but then maybe I had hoped we would meet alone," she said, looking at Bhoomi with discomfort.

"We have met Soundarya ji," Bhoomi interjected.

Soundarya was surprised to hear his voice in person. It lacked the baritone and depth when he spoke on TV debates. However, it still had the trademark accusatory tone that had made him a media poster child.

"Sure, if you say so." Soundarya nodded civilly, though her tone was icy.

"Yes, we have, Mrs Kapoor, but I guess you didn't notice me enough to remember."

"Who doesn't know you, Mr Pracharak? I remember you made me very popular."

Soundarya couldn't stand the self-conceited asshole. She gave a harried look to Meenakshi, urging her to come to the point.

"I have a preposition for you, the one which can wipe out all your problems," Meenakshi said.

"What can that be?"

"How would you feel if I told you that the government will place a large order on GCI? Not one time, but periodically assured orders."

"Why would the government buy from us?" A confused Soundarya replied.

"We will come to that later, but for now, how do you feel about it?"

"That would be something, though I would be interested to know what I have done to owe your largesse," Soundarya replied excitedly.

"You are lucky." Meenakshi smiled.

"Just that."

"For now, you need to know only that."

"As you say."

"So, if this excites you, you will have to make a part payment, a token amount, so that I can get on to work."

Soundarya nodded, looked at Bhoomi, and said, "Are you sure you want him to be here?"

"Yes, I trust him. In fact, he helped me to become Happiness Minister."

Soundarya wanted to tell her it was her problem, but kept quiet.

"How much?"

Instead of replying, Meenakshi passed a chit to Soundarya. Soundarya took it and tucked it in her LV bag.

"Let me see how soon I can do it," Soundarya said vaguely.

At this, Bhoomi raised his eyebrows and voice, "There is no time. If this doesn't happen in 24 hours, you can forget about GCI. In fact, you will be back in Azaad Nagar, where you belong."

Although he had fairly assessed her vulnerability, Soundarya turned red with indignation. But then, she would not succumb in front of an egomaniac, self-entitled man who used people as rungs of a ladder to the top.

"Mr Bhoomi, or whatever your real name is, let me tell you something. If you think you could arm-twist me, then just forget about it. I have dealt with many pimps like you in my life. I am here to meet the minister and will only speak to her."

"You seem angry," Bhoomi sneered.

"I will never give a pimp the privilege to make me angry," Soundarya said and chuckled. "I need to know some details," Soundarya addressed Meenakshi.

"Don't worry, you will know everything once you pay."

"The money will be arranged within 24 hours," Soundarya declared.

"Everything must happen fast. We need to move fast to pull it off."

"It will be done, but let me make it very clear. I don't want to ever meet this guy again. He will not be a part of any deal, now or ever," Soundarya responded, looking at Bhoomi.

Before Bhoomi could react, she reached the bar and made a large drink for herself. A confused Meenakshi also did the same.

The two ladies quickly finished their drinks and shook hands. Soundarya started to leave, but then suddenly turned around and glared at Bhoomi. "Bhoomi, tell me, do you jerk off thinking of me, you asshole?"

Bhoomi Pracharak wanted to throttle her neck, but instead, started to form a plan in his head.

Panache

Panache was a favourite of socialites and celebrities and second only to the Royal Salute in the snob index. Getting an appointment in the salon was no mean task. From its chic hairdresser chairs, luxurious spa beds and imported pedicure stations to its state-of-the-art Jacuzzis and open-air showers, everything about Panache was fashionable and expensive.

The coiffeurs, coiffeuses, manicurists, pedicurists, masseuses all were selected through a stringent process. The glamour quotient was as important as skill and mastery, and Ruchi Sharma only hired the best.

She had ignored Tanvi's messages and would have ignored them till eternity had her eyes not accidentally fallen on the last message. It was not a text but a news link captioned:

"Prostitution racket bust at massage parlour, 9 arrested, owner absconding."

As soon as she saw that, Ruchi felt a tightness in her throat, and a churning in her stomach. This was an old piece of news, over ten years old, and one she had erased from her memory and had hoped to remain buried forever. She was not the one who was absconding; it was her employer, the owner of Red Wine Spa, though she was one of the five masseuses arrested.

"Fuckin bitch," she said under her breath and gestured to her assistant to take over the cysteine treatment of a politician's wife. She hurriedly exited the salon and reached the far end of the adjoining swimming pool. Gazing at the city's smog-filled skyline, she was thinking hard.

She had been a fool to underestimate Tanvi Mehra. She should have expected that she would exploit her weakness and come after her, but then she had her reasons. Soundarya had helped her to build Panache and going against her was out of the question. She was stuck between a rock and a hard place, but now, the time had come to deal with the problem.

Hi, where, when? Let me know. Hugs, she texted back to Tanvi.

I am coming in an hour; book me for mani-pedi, pat came the reply.

An hour later, Tanvi and Ruchi sat across the mahogany table in the latter's office at the rear of the saloon. A boy served water. Tanvi took the glass, but declined his offer of coffee or tea. She was wearing a white salwar kameez and had kept her sunglasses on. To Ruchi, it appeared she was in a state of mourning.

Ruchi waited for the boy to leave the room and then said slowly, "Tanvi darling, I am very sorry about what has happened between you and Soundarya. Truth be told, I am devastated. I can't tell y—"

Tanvi waved her off before she could finish. Then she removed her glasses, looked straight into Ruchi's eyes and spoke with vehemence, "Cut the crap; I know whose side you are on, but that is your call. You could have still shown me a little courtesy by at least acknowledging my messages. Now, we are here, and you know I won't hesitate to wash your dirty linen in public, so why don't we get down to business?"

"What do you want, darling?" Ruchi asked.

"Information."

"She was here yesterday afternoon."

"In the saloon?"

"No, I saw her going up in the elevator. I think she visited someone on the fourteenth. Maybe the new Happiness Minister."

Tanvi digested the information but kept quiet.

"Anything else?"

"I believe there was some sort of meeting. Bhoomi Pracharak was also there."

"How do you know that?"

"Bhoomi is our regular, and he came down later to the spa. His favourite masseuse told me he was furious."

"Why?"

"That I am not aware of."

"Anything else, think hard."

"That's all I know, darling."

"Your information is of no use to me. How do we barter now?"

Ruchi gathered where this was going. She had a hunch that her blackmailer would eventually demand money, so why cow down?

"No, I will not. How much money do you want to settle this once and for all?" Ruchi glared back.

Tanvi wanted to slap her, but she also didn't want to say no to the money coming her way. She remembered the threatening EMI reminder. That was her immediate problem. She had taken an Uber, hoping no one would see her in the dirty hatchback.

"50 lakhs," she blurted.

Ruchi smirked and swiftly opened her locker, took out the bundles of cash, and carelessly threw them on the table.

"You obviously don't have a bag," she sneered after counting the money.

"No."

"Don't worry, I will arrange it, but you will have to pay for that."

"For what?"

"For the bag."

She pressed the bell to call the boy, who appeared in seconds and mechanically started placing the money in a jute bag. Once he finished, he handed the bag to Tanvi, who struggled to manage its weight.

"You can leave now, and if you need an appointment from now on, call the front desk, though we normally don't give appointments to people who live in *Dhobhi* Colony."

A red-faced Tanvi slowly got up from the chair and reached for the bag. As soon as her fingers touched the sling. "There's one more thing that we need to finish."

"What?"

"How do you guarantee you will not rake up this issue again?"

"You have my word," Tanvi tried to sound sincere.

"That's worthless." Ruchi laughed.

"So how?" Tanvi asked innocently.

"I will tell you how. Take off your clothes."

Eighteenth Hole

Take my breath away.

His ringtone was driving her mad. This was her tenth attempt, and just like the previous nine, the call went unanswered. Like other things, Kiku was also a slouch at receiving phone calls. It was not callousness; instead, to blame were his weak motor skills and hearing, both of which had been deteriorating over the years, though he was genetically blessed with none to start with.

He simply could never reach his pocket in time because, to do that, he had to first hear and then move his arm fast enough to grab the phone from the pocket of his ever-sagging trousers below his enormous waistline. But that was not the problem tonight. He was deliberately ignoring her calls because mother and son were huddled together on ground floor to plot against her. She was sure of that because the irritating ringtone was emanating from her mother-in-law's room.

She had texted 100 crores to Kiku soon after her meeting with Meenakshi Tandon. She could have bargained if she had not gotten distracted by Bhoomi Pracharak. Maybe she went overboard in trying to put him down but she was sure that she would not deal with him. Her father-in-law had taught her to look for telltale signs in people, and she could tell that the likes of Bhoomi were snakes who could bite anytime without warning.

The problem was that the bribe could not come out of GCI. The company was amidst a forensic audit, and most of its accounts were frozen. The other problem was that Kiku was not convinced that something like this could be pulled off. Cowards and lazies are hard-boiled cynics because, at heart, they don't want to put in the effort. But she was sure that he could be forcefully convinced.

The main issue was money. One option was to mortgage the Kapoor villa or sell off one of the many factories, the whiff of which would wipe off the remaining market cap of GCI, or it had to come from the personal account of her mother-in-law, Sumitra Kapoor. Though the first seemed suicidal, the second was difficult. Sumitra was already wealthy when she married Gulab Chand and had fiercely guarded her inheritance all her life.

Their mutual hatred was another factor. Soundarya had never really fully understood her mother-in-law's chronic dislike for her. It was not as if she had stolen her son; on the contrary, her marriage to her son was with her full approval and blessings. It was an arranged marriage.

She had wanted a simpleton bride who would forever remain subservient and grateful, and Soundarya did play the part to the extent possible. She was definitely not a fortune hunter. But at the same time, she had a life to live, and as years passed, she slowly but surely transformed from an introverted, demure woman to a society queen, a befitting title for Kapoor's *bahu*.

The first seeds of her mother-in-law's revulsion for her were sown when she developed a solid rapport with her father-in-law within the first few months of her marriage. Gulab Chand Kapoor was a hearty, mettlesome man who could charm anyone with his manners and style.

He was also an avid golfer, and once she expressed her desire to learn the game, he took her under his wings and from then on; they played a round of golf every other day for several years until the day he died of a massive heart attack on the 18th hole. Not only did her game improve with each round but also her popularity and social skills and soon, she overshadowed Sumitra Kapoor.

At that time, there were abundant rumours of her affair with her father-in-law, but all were the imagination of perverts and untrue. He was a father she never had, and for him, she was a child he had always wanted. After his unexpected death, Kiku took control of GCI, though everyone believed it was Soundarya Kapoor who was the rightful inheritor of Gulab Chand's legacy.

It was true. Gulab Chand would have given GCI to Soundarya, but for his ill-timed death, and even then, the board would have intervened if Sumitra Kapoor had not acted swiftly to crush any dissent against her son. Soundarya had accepted her fate and continued reigning over the swish social set of Victoria. But still, she kept tight control over GCI's business, waiting to make her move at the right time.

There was a possibility that her relationship with her mother-in-law would have mended. After all, Sumitra Kapoor knew her son was incapable and would eventually ruin everything, and for everyone's good, GCI should be run by Soundarya. But then, something happened that turned her dislike for her daughter-in-law into hatred.

It was sheer carelessness on Soundarya's part, a liquor-induced error of judgement that she regretted to this day. It was a cold rainy night when she came home late after a party. Late was not the issue. The issue was the man who had accompanied her.

It was an error of judgment, a grave mistake because her mother-in-law was wide awake at that hour to keep an eye on behalf of her son, who was out of town. She had tiptoed to the first floor, hid behind the glass cabinet, and had seen him enter her room.

Soundarya could have still undone the damage to some extent if she had opened the door to her mother-in-law's knocks, but she was so overcome with passion and desire that she had ignored her cries. Was it only passion and desire? No, it was as much an act of defiance. Who was she to keep tabs on her?

That was the inflexion point which had caused irreversible damage to their relationship. But that was past. GCI was dying, and she had to act fast. She called Rameshwaram and asked him to tell Kiku to come to her room immediately. Even then, the slouch took half an hour more.

She wanted to admonish him, but decided to concentrate on the task. "I met her today; she wants the money now," she said.

"How much?"

"Didn't you get my text?"

"I don't have that sort of money."

"You have nothing. Tell Sumitra it is time to sell her jewels."

"She will not agree," Kiku said in a defeated voice.

"You are the chairman, and if you can't handle her, turn over the company to me because I will manage the money."

"What is the guarantee that Meenakshi Tandon would deliver?"

"Beggars can't be choosers, it's either this or nothing. Can't you see the writing on the wall?"

Kiku threw his hands in the air in despair and started to leave the room.

"If you don't tell me by the morning, I will have to act," she shot the final warning.

The following day, Soundarya was midway through her walk when the gardener, Rohtas, came running and told her that *Maaji* was calling her to her room. She nodded but continued walking, and only once she had finished her target steps did she knock on her mother-in-law's door.

Sumitra was chanting shlokas with her eyes closed, and hearing the knock, she half opened her eyes and closed them as quickly. She completed the set of five Gayatri Mantras and lit the *dhoop agarbatti* before addressing Soundarya.

"I will give the money, provided you walk out of my son's life. I will also give you some money so you can live respectably and not have to go back to where you came from. Do we have a deal?" Sumitra said emotionlessly.

Soundarya looked at her mother-in-law. She was touching eighty with failing skin and a dithering voice and often needed a stick to walk. But even then, she was as revengeful and spiteful as she was twenty years ago. She, even now, wanted the whip. Though grudgingly, Soundarya couldn't help but admire her at that moment.

GCI had to stay afloat and to ensure that she was ready to make any sacrifice. This would be her tribute to Gulab Chand.

"Deal," she said coolly and walked away.

Breaking News

17th December

In a late-night incident, the *Dhobhi* Colony toll booth was vandalised by two unknown men. The toll collectors were severely beaten up and are presently on the life support system. The altercation started when the masked perpetrators refused to pay the toll.

Inspector Ganpule, the chief investigator, told our reporter that although these kinds of incidents at a toll booth are not uncommon, what makes this one unusual is the brutality of the attackers. Sharp razors were used to scalp chunks of skin from the faces of the victims.

The car in which the assailants came was stolen a day back. The attackers also painted the alphabet 'G' on the toll booth window. Ganpule added that there may be a new gang in town.

Ammunition

It was a rare, breathable day in December, courtesy of another unexpected downpour late at night, which rinsed the air of carbon and toxins. Tanvi was speeding, and once she hit the broad roads of Victoria, she pressed the steering mounted volume button till the speakers exploded with the compelling energy of the fifth symphony, putting her in a blissful trance.

Involuntarily, she extended her left hand to caress the soft leather upholstery and felt an intimate connection like never before. She knew why. Her beloved car was free of any encumbrance and truly hers.

After spending hours on deciding what to wear, she had finally selected a well-cut navy-blue suit that looked professional yet elegant. She wore minimal makeup except for a liberal dose of kohl. It always worked wonders for her. She may not be a classic beauty like Soundarya, and she may be a couple of shades darker, but when it came to raw sex appeal, she trounced her.

She smiled as she remembered the look on Ashok's when she told him the entire car loan was repaid in full. He had followed her like a puppy, pestering her to tell him how she did it. "None of your business," she had told him finally and had walked out of the house, twirling the key on her finger.

She knew he was not happy with this development. He was a small, manipulative man who took pleasure in others' sorrows, even if that other was his own wife. He was also embarrassed because she had again proved to him that he was no match for her. *Only if she had not hurried to marry him,* she thought and pressed hard on the accelerator with all her fury.

Another thing that was tormenting her mind was the insult she had endured at Panache. Ruchi Sharma had made her strip and taken her photos. She had relented because she didn't have any choice. It was vital to have her car back. But one day, she would make her pay back with interest, and that day, she would parade her naked in the lobby of Diplomat.

The payoff would happen soon. On reaching the Victoria Park circle, she took the third exit on a broad road flanked by jamun, Arjun and neem trees and reached her destination a hundred metres down that road. She parked her car in the lot and walked towards the imposing building.

She entered the main gate and saw a melee of people thronging the compound. There were reporters hooked to their phones, cameramen lugging their equipment, drivers sitting on charpoys and playing cards. Each news warrior was ready to reach any part of the city to break a story, even if they had to kill a few doing so. The massive signboard at the entrance read—AAM channel—Pulse of V-AN.

She had finally received a text from Bhoomi Pracharak late last night, telling her to meet him at his office. After what Ruchi had told her, she had a gut feeling that something was going on. Why would Soundarya Kapoor meet the just appointed Happiness Minister? She knew that despite GCI's proclamations that media reports about its financials were smoke and mirrors, a witch hunt, GCI was in trouble.

Even if she discounted the reports, there were other telltale signs since the past few months—Soundarya was repeating dresses, had not thrown a party for a while, and was easily irritable, far removed from her usual confident self. But how was this connected to Meenakshi Tandon?

After tearing her hair over it for hours, she had reconciled that only Bhoomi Pracharak could unravel the plot, so she had obtained his number from a contact and persistently messaged him till he had replied.

She took the elevator to the top floor and approached Bhoomi's secretary's desk. The attractive girl first looked through her, and then absentmindedly asked her to wait. Reluctantly, Tanvi joined the long queue of visitors and recognised a few politicians and businessmen. There were obvious reasons for the long line.

TRP apart, the AAM channel was powerful because it turned the news into debates and debates into verdicts, delivered by its owner and chief editor. But no one was complaining. Entertainment-hungry citizens lapped up everything. In any case, who wanted boring facts over unsubstantiated racy reports?

To kill time, Tanvi took a selfie and posted it on Insta with #shiningatwork and then got busy counting likes, which soon turned out to be a depressing occupation because of the low count and the revelation that Soundarya and many members of M&S had blocked her.

She was on the brink of another mental collapse when she was finally ushered into Bhoomi's office after an hour's wait. He didn't acknowledge her presence and continued reading papers on his desk for what felt like an eternity to her. She was on tenterhooks and was fast losing hope before he finally spoke.

"Why were you so desperate to meet me?" He asked roughly.

For a moment, Tanvi was taken aback by the line of questioning, but soon recovered. She was dealing with a professional bully, and she needed to have her wits about.

She looked straight into his eyes and said, "I need ammunition."

"For what?"

"To destroy our common enemy."

Bhoomi took out his glasses and looked amused. "Whom are you referring to?"

"You know that. Her name was in my message you finally responded to," Tanvi replied in a witty voice.

"Why would I help you?" Bhoomi threw the papers aside and directly looked at her eyes.

"Because our goals are the same."

Bhoomi waited a few moments and then replied in a condescending tone, "You are too small a fish."

Tanvi was unmoved. "I don't think you think that. I am sure you made inquiries about me before agreeing to meet. You are a busy man."

"And you are an extortionist."

So, he did speak to Ruchi, Tanvi felt a rush of excitement.

Bhoomi continued, "I called you here because your reputation precedes you. You have the attributes required for this job, cunningness and ambition, but more than that, it is your quest for revenge, the primordial force that can move mountains, and that's why you are standing here."

"So, give me a lead," Tanvi asked firmly.

"Do you know that your friend is bankrupt?"

"I have an idea, but then she has assets. The Kapoor villa itself is worth several crores, and they have so many factories."

"All will be taken away soon and Kapoors will be on the street. But then, there is a plan in motion which can save her. All you have to do is disrupt that plan."

"I am confused. Can you please be clear?"

Instead of answering her, Bhoomi got up from his chair, came around the table and stood behind Tanvi. He then put his hands on her shoulder and brought his mouth close to her ears, and spoke in a hushed voice. An hour later, the two were going through each step of the plan.

"You will have the support of the opposition and others. The only thing you have to do is get him to Victoria Park," Bhoomi said.

"I will leave tomorrow," replied an eager Tanvi.

"All your travel arrangements have been made."

Tanvi was instantly surprised. That meant her 'yes' to the plan was taken for granted, and why not? This plan could not only get her revenge but also could change her destiny forever.

"What is in it for you, apart from your hatred for Soundarya Kapoor? Aren't you close to Siddheshwar Gupta?" She couldn't help but ask.

"GKP is a sinking ship, irrespective of whatever they come up with. The drama you will create will send my TRP through the roof. So, you see, it's also my greed."

Ghatak Gang

Getting into her house was not all that difficult for him. Her landlord, who was also his father, kept a duplicate key tied to the *nada* of his pyjamas. Lovely had waited till midnight, and only when he was sure that his old man was comatose after consuming a bottle of country liquor that he had disrobed him.

Though he felt miserable in the act, he had no option. Removing the key from his *nada* while he was wearing the pyjamas was risky, even though it was unlikely that even a fire could awaken the drunk. He had quickly pulled out the key and then spread the pyjama on his creator's bare genitals.

Her house was dark, and as he moved forward, his thumb hit the leg of the sofa. *Behenchod,* he wailed and sat on the sofa, waiting for the excruciating pain to subside. Later, he switched on the light and took a deep breath to soak in the smell of her perfume mixed with the cigarette stench hanging in the air.

He belonged there. Technically also, he was the heir of the house and the *paan* shop once his father died, which he guessed would be soon, because of diabetes or herpes. He could tell Ashok was fast asleep from the loud snores and wheezing from the bedroom. Still, he latched the bedroom door from outside just in case.

Fuckin' loser. How could someone with a wife like that ever sleep? He would not catch a wink if he was in his place, fearing losing moments with her. He checked his watch. It was 12.30 pm, and by observing her movements for the past year, he knew Tanvi Mehra never returned home before 2.

He could catch some sleep on the sofa; instead, he decided to make good use of the time. He started spot-jumping to warm up. Ten minutes later, he got on all fours and did 50 push-ups. He needed to be in top shape for her, so he followed it up with a ten minutes plank. Half an hour later, he was weary and angry.

How could she make him wait? Angrily, he opened the bottle of whisky he had got for her. He had extorted it from the neighbouring liquor shop, promising protection in return. That's what godfathers did. They earned goodwill through their deeds. He had seen the movie a hundred times and swooned by the Marlon Brando's restrained menace, his style and, above all, his sense of justice. The entire *Dhobhi* Colony may call him a loafer, but one day, he would show them his worth. He would be their godfather.

He took a large gulp straight from the bottle. It bothered him that he was consuming from the bottle he was to gift her, but the damn thing was so tempting, and wasn't she the one making him wait or else they would have been drinking together.

The alcohol relaxed him. He was in the house of his lover, who had bared for him. His only regret was that night; instead of him, *Gandu* was beneath her. He wished no harm to Ashok Mehra as long as he quietly moved out of her life. He would also be fair and reasonable in return, just like Godfather would. As the hubris hit him, he took another gulp; this time, twice the quantity of liquor entered his body, and he found himself in another world.

They were walking towards Terminal 3, he, in a black suit and aviator glasses, and she, in a black camisole and fitted jeans that hugged her long legs. A battery of cameramen on both sides of the railing were trying to capture a shot of them. He nodded to the onlookers and presented his boarding pass at the gate. The security guard scanned his pass and asked him to wait.

"You want to die?" Lovely threatened.

"I can't let you in," the man said and shrugged his shoulders.

Lovely took out his pistol and was about to fire when a group of men in black suits caught him and started dragging him. Brutally overpowered, he helplessly saw another group of men hauling his girlfriend to a police van parked nearby.

He wanted to kill everyone, but was helpless. Tears started flowing from his face, and he yelled, "Leave her or else you all would die!"

Suddenly, he felt a jolt on his shoulder and opened his eyes in panic. She was standing right there. Her clothes were intact, and her face was fine except for a frown. He felt so relieved that he wanted to get up and hug her; instead, he closed his eyes again.

"What are you doing here?" Tanvi slapped his shoulder.

Lovely slowly opened his eyes and sheepishly got up from the sofa. He picked up the half-empty whisky bottle from the table and extended his arm.

"I got this for you."

"Empty bottle."

"Half-empty. I drank a little while waiting for you."

"Did you get a soda?"

"Yes, it's here," he said eagerly, pointing to the polythene bag.

"Make my drink."

An embarrassed Lovely went to the kitchen and got a glass for her. He made a drink for both of them, pouring only a few drops for himself. *Why did he fall asleep?* He cursed himself. He had ruined his impression.

"I have left school," he barely managed to mumble.

"What do you plan to do?" She asked with amusement.

"I have started a business."

"What business?"

"I am the founder of the Ghatak gang."

"What's that?"

"Did you hear what happened on *Dhobhi* Colony toll? Ghatak did it."

When she heard that, she felt a spine-chilling sensation. The gory details of the incident were all over the news. She wondered how this guy could do it. She took an uncomfortable sip while looking for telltale signs and noticed the veins jutting out from his forearms and callous-filled hands. She knew he was a strong, handsome lad who would end up as a local thug, but she had never imagined that he would be such a ferocious fiend.

He could be useful.

She raised her glass. "Cheers."

Lovely suddenly made a comeback. This was how he had wanted their relationship to progress—a relationship based on mutual respect. He didn't want to waste time expressing his feelings for her in words. He had seen in movies that white people expressed their love with a lip lock. He also wanted to do the same.

He took quick steps towards her, took the glass from her hand and bent to kiss her.

"Wait," she said as soon as their lips were about to meet.

"What's the problem?" Lovely asked.

"I have got lots on my mind."

"Tell me."

"If I tell you, would you help me?"

"From now on, your problems are my problems."

The Den

Soundarya didn't want the meeting to take place at Diplomat. The last time, she was spotted, despite the entire charade of secrecy. Also, visiting a suite in Diplomat was painful. It reminded her of the halcyon days of GCI, now only a blip in her memory.

She wanted a remote place this time, and a friend's farmhouse on the city's outskirts seemed the best option. When she suggested the venue to Meenakshi, she was reluctant at first. Politicians have big egos, and it was only when Soundarya told her about the grandeur of the farmhouse and that she would even organise horse riding for her that Meenakshi agreed. Both the ladies drove separately; Soundarya was the first to reach and Meenakshi, half an hour later.

"Same pinch," Soundarya cheerfully said to Meenakshi as soon as she alighted from her car. Meenakshi was confused until Soundarya told her they wore the same shade of Burberry jeans. They pleasantly shook hands and proceeded to the Spanish ranch-style bungalow. The farm's owner was not present, and it was only the two of them and a dozen staff members to take care of them.

"Let's go to the den," Soundarya suggested and guided Meenakshi through a long glass-panelled passageway bisecting the swimming pool.

The so-called den was tastefully done with comfy green sofas, fancy rugs, a well-stocked wine cooler, modern art on walls, and lots of leather. A pungent smell of cigars was hanging in the air.

"Champagne?" Soundarya asked, and Meenakshi gave a nod.

A minute later, the two were savouring their drink amidst small talk. Soundarya asked Meenakshi about her years abroad and how she was finding life in the city.

"Even though I was born and brought up here, I find everything so unfamiliar now. I constantly feel anxious. Maybe it's because of my job, or maybe it's the tension in the air," Meenakshi shared.

"Yes, this city can get on the nerves, but again, it depends. I was born into extreme poverty in Azaad Nagar. When I started living in Victoria after my marriage, it was a dream come true, a dream I am living to this day."

"Oh yes, it would have been a life-changing experience for you. I can well imagine how exciting this transition would have been. With me, there was no such thing. My father was an IAS officer, and I lived in Victoria. I guess when one has an entitled background, one does tend to lose the fire in the belly."

Although Soundarya kept a poker face, she didn't like the way Meenakshi said that. She was covertly insulting her. But then, it was always the case. For whatever she had achieved, she was always looked down upon by born rich, though most were scared to say it openly. So, they would talk about her amazing transition from poor to rich, but never forget to mention her lowly origins. Soundarya was fed up and was not ready to bear it any longer.

"If you have no fire in the belly, why are you corrupt?"

This stung Meenakshi; her face turned red, and she emptied her glass in few large gulps.

"Let's talk business," she said curtly.

"Your fee has been wired," Soundarya gave back.

"If you say so, I haven't checked." It was a lie.

"You can check; now is the time for you to deliver."

Meenakshi looked hassled and arched her eyebrow.

"Don't worry about that, but there is one more condition."

"What condition?"

"TWW will also be part of the deal."

"No way, we have paid."

"And they have paid double what you have paid."

"What do you mean TWW will be the part? It is a foreign company. Also, their products are expensive, and there is no way they can win against us even if there is a tender."

"You are right. They can't win on their own, but there is one way it can be a win-win for all."

"How?"

"They will buy GCI."

Suddenly, everything became clear to Soundarya. A middleman had approached her a couple of months ago with a plan to rescue GCI, and selling came up on the table. Then, out of the blue, Bear Investments came up with the report, and GCI stock plummeted. Soon after, the same middleman arranged the meeting between GCI and TWW. Nothing was coincidental. There were larger forces at play.

"What if I say no? To hell with your plan," Soundarya snarled.

"You like it or not, this marriage will take place," Meenakshi said firmly.

"Kiku will not agree. You would know what has happened between him and Robert Brown. My husband is egoistic and would never agree to such an arrangement."

"That is for you to deal with, but let me explain my logic. Regardless of what happens in the future, GCI will lose. If you take the deal, you will not only mitigate that risk but also get all the money and a significant stake in TWW. Also, you can extract more price once a large government order is awarded to GCI. Think rationally. I have heard of your many qualities, and pragmatism is one of them. A pragmatic businessman always cuts a deal."

Though Soundarya was incensed, she could see the reason. But then there was a problem.

"I am sure Kiku will not agree."

"That is for you to deal with; like I said, I consider you the boss."

"When are you moving?"

"Very fast. Tomorrow is the meeting. I need the answer now. What I will do will change your fortune."

"I hate to be hurried, but I will call you." Soundarya got up to leave the room. Her mind was racing, and she was in no mood to entertain Meenakshi any further.

When one has to pay the full price, there is no point in pursuing the seller.

As for Kiku, there was only one way to convince him.

"I will wait for your confirmation," Meenakshi said and walked off.

Scissor Steps

That morning, for the first time in his life, Kiku Kapoor woke up before the alarm. Surprisingly, there was no migraine, an affliction he had suffered since childhood. Something had definitely changed in the last twenty-four hours. He felt energetic, almost restless and also light-headed. His appetite for junk and booze had also reduced, and he felt like a new man, ready for a fresh chapter in life.

In the next half hour, he got ready for the session in his orange Lululemon tracksuit and matching sneakers. He leaned on the terrace ledge, anticipating her arrival, and saw Soundarya briskly walking on the lawn. He called out her name, but she didn't respond. Maybe because of the ear pods, he reasoned to himself, then took his mind off his wife's ignorance and started moving his body energetically to warm up. Today, he was going to impress Malaika.

A few minutes later, the creak of the main gate made his heart skip a beat. He ran towards the edge and saw Malaika resplendent in black racerback and matching capri sweatpants. Her hair was tied in a bun with a red band, and the white framed Fendi sunglasses he had gifted her covered half of her small face.

She was as cool as the young girls he was used to seeing dancing at the Royal Salute. What he liked most were her arms—thin with just a hint of muscles, her breasts—just the right size, and her nose ring he suspected she had started wearing since their last session to tease him. He liked petite and slim, probably because he had been ridiculed for being large and fat all his life.

He waved at her, and she waved back with a broad grin. Then she abruptly turned and walked up to Soundarya. Kiku panicked momentarily, wondering why she was doing that, but when he saw both smiling and talking, he calmed down quickly. It was great that both the females in his life had good relations with each other.

One thing that he had always credited Soundarya with was her maturity. They may not be in love in the classical sense, but there was enough chemistry between them to let each other live. He was also aware of her flings, but had never reacted, and he now expected the same from her.

He and Soundarya had fought after she had told him that as part of the deal brokered by Meenakshi Tandon, TWW would buy out GCI at forty a share. He had told her in no uncertain terms that he would rather die than agree to such an arrangement. Forty was a reasonable price and one he would have agreed to before that meeting. But not now.

He preferred hunger than selling his company to a person who had beaten him in public. Whatever happened to GCI, he was not ready to shake hands with Robert Brown and forgive the insolent bastard. He also wanted Soundarya's support to counter the hostile takeover of GCI.

After all, she was also a Kapoor, the one groomed by the great Gulab Chand, who had neglected his son but showed love for his daughter-in-law. Sometimes, he wondered if the rumours about his father and his wife were true. It had caused him much pain and embarrassment then, but now, it didn't matter as he was in love himself.

His love for her was different. Probably, it was infatuation in the beginning and maybe lust, but now all he felt for her was love and affection. Though he was physically attracted to her, he wanted to suppress that feeling because he first wanted her to fall in love with him.

Still, from time to time, he thought of her as he was doing right now, and suddenly, his heart fluttered. That was also something that had been happening for the last two days. He was taking his meds on time, but he could feel his heart beating faster several times a day.

Maybe that's what happens when one falls in love!

Malaika had also become his closest confidant. A kind-hearted, mature girl who had gently comforted him after his fight with Brown. She had made him do deep breathing, which had put him at peace. After a few drinks, he had shared his innermost secrets with her, and she had listened patiently and given some excellent advice. In the end, she had taken his hand in hers and promised him that she would always be there for him. He had finally found his intellectual and spiritual companion at fifty.

Let GCI wind up. His mother had enough money of her own, which he would eventually inherit. He could afford the same lifestyle, and nothing else mattered with Malaika by his side.

Excitedly, he broke into the dance step he had tried to learn last night from YouTube. Malaika was fond of dancing, and he had promised her he would also become a decent dancer. One day, they would dance together at Royal Salute, and the ground would slip underneath his detractors. Lost in thoughts, he excitedly fist-punched the air.

"Hey, someone looks all fresh and ready," Malaika said as soon as she stepped onto the terrace.

Kiku gave an embarrassed smile, like the teacher had just rewarded him for finishing homework. She took the Bluetooth speaker from her bag and paired it with her phone. Soon enough, 'Eye of the Tiger' started blasting from the Bose speaker.

"Today, we are going to do high-intensity interval training. It's called HIIT, and it is the best calorie burner. Are you up to it?"

"Yes, yes," he said, jumping nervously on the spot.

"The first move is alternating toe touches, count of 30."

Facing each other, they started the exercise, though Kiku could barely touch his knees, let alone toe.

"*Un deux trois,* change. Scissor steps, count of 30."

He followed her command and started moving his legs forward and back. Fitness was his life's mission now.

"3, 2, 1, change. Step walks over, count of 30."

He was sweating from all pores but followed her steps.

"*Un deux trois,* change. Jumping jacks, count of 30."

He forgot the crushing pain in his legs and started jumping vigorously.

It's the eye of the tiger; it's the thrill of the fight, the speaker roared.

"3, 2, 1, change. Mountain climber, count of 30."

Though the pounding of his heart could be heard a mile away, he followed her instructions. He had to prove that he was worthy of her.

It was do or die.

"Another set of all three," she thundered.

They continued for another ten minutes, and at some point, nausea hit him. He wanted to tell Malaika to stop, but couldn't. The words would not come out of his mouth; instead, what came out was a whole lot of phlegm laced with blood.

"Let's do stretching and finish for the day; we will do your favourite back *wali,*" she said, deliberately not looking at him.

Call an ambulance. His lips moved, but the words didn't come out.

He was desperately hoping that she would read his lips. His arms had no strength to even touch her. Instead, she held him and turned him around, entangled her arms with his and lifted him. He laughed at first. Then, there was a loud grunt. He took several rapid breaths, followed by no breathing. Then he was breathing again.

For the next minute or so, she could feel his breathing deepening at intervals and then getting shallower and shallower. If she could see his face, she would know it was devoid of colour, but she could feel his cold arms. She started sobbing. It was another minute before she released him and ran without turning back.

Midway down the stairs, she bumped into Soundarya. Their eyes met, but none spoke. A few seconds later, Soundarya stood beside his body. His eyes and jaw were wide open as rigour mortis had set in.

"Oh my god," Soundarya said involuntarily and broke down into fits of tears. The sharp sense of grief weakened her legs, and she fell down next to him. Moments later, she touched his face with her palm. As soon as she did that, he suddenly drew air and gasped, and his body twitched. Soundarya jerked backwards in panic.

Their eyes met for a fraction of a second, and then he went pale. Soundarya walked away, but not before sending a message to Meenakshi Tandon:

'We have a deal.'

And the last known survivor stalks his prey in the night—the music continued.

Cabinet Meeting

19th December

The agenda for the cabinet meeting was flashing on the screen: Agenda: To discuss and finalise measure(s) for improvement in the Happiness Index.

7.00 pm: Presentation by Happiness Minister.

7.30 pm: Proposals by Happiness Minister.

7.30-8 pm: Brainstorming.

8.15 pm: Decision.

8.30 pm: Cocktails and Dinner (Hotel Diplomat).

The cocktails were Meenakshi's idea to ensure a hundred per cent attendance, not because she had underestimated her fellow ministers' resourcefulness to manage free liquor, evening after evening. It was because she reckoned that drinking in the garb of a serious intellectual mind fuck that too during a cabinet meeting, would be tempting to most.

She was right. Except for Deputy CM Banke Singh, all were seated in the Durbar Hall dot at 7 pm. Siddheshwar didn't want to wait for a second for his second-in-command, so he signalled Meenakshi to commence.

"Please start, Meenakshi," he said impatiently from the head of the rectangular conference table. Meenakshi was seated to his left, and the chair on his right was left vacant for Banke.

Meenakshi stood up, adjusted her spectacles, and pouted her mouth to blow a few strands of her hair that had fallen on her face. She was holding papers in her left hand, and her right hand was clutching the seam of her beige saree. She momentarily closed her eyes to concentrate and spoke with a slight accent.

"Respected CM Sir and my colleagues, since taking over as Happiness Minister, I have done nothing other than trying hard to figure out how we can make our people happy in the shortest possible time. But the first thing is to understand what happiness is?"

With that, she pressed a button, and a question came on the screen:

What is Happiness?

She paused briefly to let it sink into her audience and then continued slowly, like a lecturer, "The dictionary informs us that happiness means a state of well-being and contentment. It is a somewhat complex and nuanced definition that probably only an intellectual or a psychiatrist can understand. The citizens also know this, which is why they are cynical about my appointment as Happiness Minister.

"Since the day of my appointment, I have been brutally trolled, and many perverts are openly demanding a happy ending from me. After deliberating these over endless hours, I have concluded that if this is what it means, it is an impossible task. It is not measurable and depends on factors beyond the control of an elected government. A government cannot play any role in making people happy," she concluded, making many, including Siddheshwar Gupta, wonder if she was about to quit.

Siddheshwar was already regretting agreeing with her in the first place and making her the Happiness Minister. His reputation was already in shambles, and now this hara-kiri would ensure he went down in the history books as the worst CM ever. He felt a longing for a drink and was about to get up when she began speaking again, this time in a clear and confident voice.

"That brings me to another definition of happiness. Happiness is also a pleasurable and satisfying experience. Here also, satisfaction is something unquantifiable, but pleasure is more tangible, and pleasure is something I want to work on. So, in a nutshell, providing pleasure to citizens is the easiest and surest way to bring happiness in their lives." She pressed the key to change the slide, and now it read:

Happiness = Pleasure

"Let's organise your dance in every nook and corner of the state for everyone's pleasure."

All heads turned towards Banke Singh, who had joined the meeting at some point and was grinning from ear to ear.

But then his grin faded away quickly as Meenakshi rebutted, "Bankeji, it is no secret that you are happiest when you dance and sleep with young men from your village. Now, I was not talking about that kind of happiness."

"Jaban sambhal ke aurat." Banke's face exploded with anger, and using the enormous power of his hips, he sent his chair flying backwards and then jumped on the table with extended arms to catch Meenakshi's neck. In the process, his left foot hit Siddheshwar Gupta's face, and the right hit the health minister, who had been a renowned orthopaedic before joining politics.

Meenakshi swiftly took a few steps back, then pointed her phone and clicked pictures of Banke sprawled on the table, his eyes gouging out and his mouth ready to bite.

At that point, someone in the cabinet had the mind to shout for Marshalls posted outside the Durbar Hall. Within seconds, four of them entered Durbar Hall, wearing traditional warrior dresses with a *pagdi* atop. On the CM's direction, they lifted Banke from the table and carried him out of the hall. During his journey from Durbar

Hall to his car, Banke kept shouting choicest expletives addressed to Meenakshi Tandon.

Only after Banke's shouts became a distant whisper was there a collective sigh of relief in the room.

"That was not required," Siddheshwar said sternly while wiping the dust of Banke's sandals from his cheek. The flying kick from his deputy had given him a sudden headache, and he was worried that it would have caused permanent damage to his nut.

"You know the man. He would have killed me. I will send these pictures to the press and let the law take its own course—you all are witnesses of how he tried to kill me—fucker will be behind bars for the rest of his life," Meenakshi replied agitatedly.

"For god's sake, Meenakshi, please cool down," Siddheshwar said, and then he looked at the others. "None of this goes out of the Durbar Hall."

"What about the Marshalls?" The law minister asked, scratching his chin.

"Brief them, tell them they will lose their job under Official Secrets Act if any of them opens their mouth," Siddheshwar thundered. "And also, all of you, nothing goes out, or I will personally fuck the happiness of anyone who leaks this."

"And that applies to you too, Meenakshi," he added.

"Don't you sympathise with my situation?" Meenakshi said, her voice now resonating with her pain.

"I do, and justice will be served, but for now, please concentrate on the task at hand," Siddheshwar pleaded.

"I need to freshen up first," Meenakshi said, and abruptly left the room in quick paces.

She returned after fifteen minutes, during which Siddheshwar Gupta's cabinet and he kept fiddling with papers, pretending they were busy. In reality, most of them were trying to control their laughter, except for the two victims of Banke's kick—the CM and the health minister. Still, all managed to keep a straight face.

Meenakshi returned, looking fresh but sullen. Siddheshwar felt sympathy for her. If he had had his way, he would have put Banke behind bars, but a scandal of this nature could ruin even the slightest chance of winning the elections. Sometimes, one had to compromise to meet a more important objective.

"Ok, where was I?" Meenakshi said; suddenly, she was all professional.

"Pleasure," someone murmured cautiously.

"Yes. Pleasure is an integral part of happiness, which I intend to work on."

She suddenly smiled and changed the slide:

Pleasure—getting something good or much wanted.

"Now, there are many ways to provide pleasure to our citizens. We could simply transfer money into their bank accounts or give them tickets to travel the world. But all these things are expensive for our cash-strapped state and, at best, are a one-time affair. What we need is to provide them with a daily dose of measured happiness, so that they remain forever indebted to us."

"Free yoga camps?" The health minister said unconvincingly.

"Box of sweets?" The food minister suggested.

Meenakshi looked furtively at Siddheshwar, who seemed to be in deep thought.

"Bullshit ideas will not do anything to change the fortunes of GKP because none will provide instant gratification or pleasure. Yoga will be punishment for most, and *ladoos* are not a drug. What we need is a drug," she said.

"What exactly do you have in mind?" Siddheshwar asked while scratching his head to try to foresee where this was going.

"Let me ask you a question, Sid. What makes you happy? What gives you pleasure?"

Siddheshwar was irritated by the question, but then closed his eyes to think. When he spoke, he sounded unsure, "There are many things, like when I do something good, it gives me happiness or when I listen to music or watch a good movie or eat a fine meal."

"Maybe sometimes, but tell me something accessible and sure to pleasure you."

Before the CM could respond, Meenakshi clapped her hands, and a couple of waiters entered the Durbar Hall in pristine white uniforms. In their hands were trays containing liquor and glasses. Everyone in the room was perplexed; still, at the same time, a visible glow appeared on everyone's face. The waiters quietly served drinks to everyone and left.

Nobody moved till Meenakshi lifted her glass and said, "Cheers."

Everyone reluctantly followed except for Siddheshwar Gupta, who kept staring at Meenakshi.

"So, is this your plan?"

"Yes, it is, and it will work. I have no doubt in my mind."

"Where is the money?"

"A liquor company is ready to support the government for at least a few months. They will not take payment upfront."

"And after that?"

"We will figure something out when you get elected."

"What do they want in return?"

"Nothing."

"But how will it happen? Is it even legal?"

"Was electricity free anywhere? You came up with it because you are never afraid to break the status quo."

"How much?"

"180 ml per person per day."

"How did you come at this figure?"

"I commissioned a study by experts."

"Doctors?"

"No, boozards who drink daily. They are part of the tribe who call themselves daily passengers. No one can be a bigger expert than them."

"Both men and women?"

"Yes, how can there be gender discrimination in this?" Meenakshi did not hide her irritation.

"Sorry I asked. For those who don't drink?"

"Milk in lieu."

"Why will any company support it?"

"Because this one has no other option. It will be a big order for them, and they also know that no one will stop at 180 ml, so they will have more sales."

"Which company?"

"GCI."

"You mean Gulaabo?"

"Yes, the queen of good times."

Alcoholism

"Ours was a movement against corruption, which has plagued politics, business and society. Five years back, we were on the verge of success when my right hand, whom I considered my son, backstabbed me and got into politics. To make it worse, after becoming the chief minister, he embraced all the sins we were fighting against."

Tanvi saw tears in his eyes and pain in his voice. It was true that a lot had changed in those five years, including his physical condition. Then, Guruji was an energetic man who could evoke strong emotions in his countless supporters through his speeches and actions. Now, he was just a shadow of his past self and looked weak and fragile.

Was it ethical to get him embroiled in politics again for self-serving purposes? She had asked herself several times on her way from the airport to his village, which turned out to be an arduous eight-hour journey on potholed roads. Having hardly slept for the past twenty-four hours, she was physically tired, and the persistent nagging of her conscience had also tired her mentally. But then she kept telling herself that her mission was far too important to jeopardise for physical discomfort and newfound guilt.

She had to give the performance of her life.

Guilt could wait.

Guruji agreed to meet her when she cried on the phone while telling him what the government was planning to do. Now, she was face to face with him in a sparsely furnished, nondescript room whose walls needed painting and the floor needed plastering. The most prominent fixture in the room was the garlanded portrait of the 'Father of the Nation'. Overall, it was the modest abode of a man who had single-handedly brought down a government and had brought corruption in high places to the attention of the masses.

Someone gave her water in a steel glass corroded at the rim. She hesitated to drink from it, but she drank it when she felt Guruji's eyes gauging her reaction. For everything to succeed, Guruji needed to have implicit trust in her.

After moments of silence, Tanvi spoke softly, "Guruji, I understand your disappointment, but we cannot let the tyrant have his own way just to win the forthcoming elections. We need to stop him for the sake of our future generations."

She noticed Guruji was studying her face and seemed unsure of her intentions.

"Why are you here, *beta*? You are an urban woman with sensibilities, unlike those of an old man like me. Why are you so passionate about the cause?" He finally spoke.

Tanvi had many reasons to be there, but she needed to come up with the right one. As the question was expected, she had rehearsed the answer.

"Guruji, I am a victim of alcoholism. My father was an alcoholic, and so was my husband. They ruined my life, and now I have made it my mission to save millions from ruining their lives."

Accusing her husband was the most difficult part of that answer. It would have been game over if she had laughed at that instant, remembering Ashok Mehra arranging sodas for her and making her large ones. So, she clasped her hands tightly to control, but the tears flowed, which she hoped Guruji would take as tears of sorrow.

"I am not well."

"What happened, Guruji?" Tanvi said in a concerned voice.

"The doctor says my blood sugar is very low, and fasting can further deteriorate the condition."

This was the ultimate test of her conscience. She was instantly torn and on the verge of giving up till she remembered how just a week back, she was humiliated and thrown out of the party, that too, on her birthday. Her subsequent removal from the group had momentarily killed her will to live. She was still alive, hoping that she would get even one day. If she gave up now, it would be suicide, and only cowards committed suicide, and Tanvi Mehra may be anything but a coward.

"Guruji, I will personally make sure that nothing happens to you. I am like your daughter. No daughter would let her father suffer. We will have the best medical facilities and, in any case, this will last for up to a couple of days. The entire state is waiting for you with bated breath."

Having thrown the only ace in her pack, she could now just pray. Guruji left without replying and entered the adjoining room. The wait was long, and Tanvi sat there nervously, twitching her hands and feet. Guruji's no would mean the end of the road for her. At last, she heard his footsteps and her heart raced. Guruji emerged with a *potli* in his hand.

Chalo beta.

Breaking News

21st December

FLS to be implemented soon.

It is learnt from reliable sources that the Free Liquor Scheme (FLS), similar to FEWS, will soon be rolled out by the GKP government. There is no official confirmation, and the emails sent have been unanswered.

The opposition spokesperson Bhure Prasad has said they will approach the court as a scheme such as FLS cannot be implemented just before the elections. When asked what he thinks about FLS, he said that he won't be able to comment till such time the details of the scheme are known.

The shares of liquor companies rallied today. In particular, the shares of GCI hit the upper circuit, with speculation, that the queen of good times—Gulaabo will be the chosen under FLS.

Guruji is back.

Guruji has arrived in Victoria. There are strong speculations in the political circles and media that this is in response to the FLS, and he will soon start fasting at Victoria Park. If that happens, the state will witness a repeat of what happened five years back.

Happiness Minister resigns.

In a surprising development, the newly appointed Happiness Minister has resigned. She has already left for the US, where she intends to pursue her academic career. This is surprising because it is widely believed that FLS is the brainchild of Meenakshi Tandon.

Kiku Kapoor dies.

Kiku Kapoor, chairman of GCI, died in the early hours today due to a massive heart attack while exercising. It is ironic, as GCI is likely to be the biggest beneficiary of FLS.

***

FLS

File No: XXX/FLS/GLB
22 December

To,

The citizens of Victoria and Azaad Nagar (V-AN)
Dear citizens,

I have the pleasure of conveying the orders of Shri Siddheshwar Gupta, Honourable Chief Minister, but before I come to that, I would like to give you some background.

Modern life is stressful. While, on one hand, the human race is reaping the benefits of rapid development, on the other hand, it is also paying the price for it. It is observed that the happiness of our citizens has been the single big casualty as our great state marches ahead.

A sensitive government has its ears on the ground. It is sensitive to the needs of its citizens and moves mountains to provide them with what they want. As you are aware, a new Happiness Ministry was created a few days back, the first of its kind in the world. It is a testimony of the unique model of governance of the incumbent government, just like the Free Electricity and Water scheme (FEWS) already in force.

The Happiness Ministry has come up with its recommendations. They have recommended a controlled dose of an antidote to each eligible citizen of V-AN, which will help reduce stress and sorrow and increase happiness. The CM has accepted the recommendations.

With this (I urge you to hold your breath), I announce the roll-out of the Free Liquor Scheme (FLS) from 1 January.

Operating instructions:

- The FLS quota is 180 ml/day of Gulaabo rum for all citizens above 18.
- The scheme is voluntary, and if someone wishes to opt out for any reason (moral or otherwise), give a missed call on our toll-free number 1800-000-000 and leave your name and Aadhar number.
- If a citizen is a teetotaller, they can fill out an online form on www.fls.com and opt for 1 litre of milk instead.
- The FLS quota will be home delivered along with rations.
- The scheme will be reviewed after three months.

Moral and Miscellaneous Instructions:

- It is recommended that the entire family drink together in a congenial environment.
- No one should exceed the 180 ml quota because the research points out that anything in excess may in fact reduce happiness.
- Soothing music will be played on the Doordarshan and Vividh Bharati between 8 to 9 pm, and all are advised to listen to the same while drinking.
- Citizens are advised not to get into arguments while enjoying their drinks.
- Drinking and driving are prohibited as before.

Signed
PK Talli
Chief Secretary

Gabru

Zaalim teri ankh main
Hath dal kar
Teri ankh noch lenge
Teri ankh noch lenge
noch lenge noch lenge noch lenge noch lenge.

As the notes reached a crescendo, Gabru started head banging and thrusting his crotch towards the crowd, triggering waves of hysteria. When his audience responded fervently to *noch lenge,* he flung his metal-studded jacket into the crowd, exposing his bare chest full of tattoos, the most prominent of which was the bald eagle—a symbol of strength, courage, freedom and immortality.

As he danced to the beat of the drums, his golden hair swayed left and right like a boat caught in a temper, and his jeans inched dangerously low. Tanvi got nervous at seeing the antics. If the jeans slipped a few centimetres more, it may result in a controversy that could sabotage the movement. But she was helpless, and Gabru was too stoned to care.

Guruji had started his fast until death that morning, barely 24 hours after the announcement on FLS. In his opening speech, Guruji called it the *Nashabandi* movement, which made the organisers extremely uncomfortable. The word *Nashabandi* (prohibition) was dangerously close to *Nasbandi* (sterilisation), and as such, espousing a blanket ban on liquor would be political suicide.

So, they pleaded with Guruji, who reluctantly agreed to call it just *Andolan* (revolution).

The crowds had started pouring into Victoria Park before sunrise. Their conveyance (buses and tractors) was arranged by the opposition and the Bear cartel, which had short positions in GCI stock. In fact, the whole show—shamiana, food, DJ, and lighting—was sponsored by those two and some unnamed parties.

Tanvi Mehra was appointed the chief coordinator of the movement and was entrusted with planning all activities. Getting a moody and eccentric Gabru to perform was a coup because making a splash on the first day was critical. The people of V-AN had witnessed Guruji's fast five years back, and the repeat performance, notwithstanding the reason, would be stale.

Gabru was the country's current darling and had a big fan following. To top it off, he mostly sang anti-establishment songs, enticing people to take on weapons against injustice. Except that he was a drug addict fighting a manslaughter case, he was a perfect choice. He was also a thief who stole lyrics and music with utter disdain.

Nonetheless, seeing him in action, Tanvi beamed at her decision. It was seven in the evening, and the temperature had dipped below 10 degrees, but for Guruji's supporters, it was a party. The circular road surrounding the VC park perimeter was jam-packed, caused mainly by the media vans.

Also, plenty of hawkers sold peanuts, boiled eggs, momos and ice cream to the captive crowd. There were also jeeps parked in a nearby lane, packed with liquor to be given as a bribe to protestors. No one felt anything odd about it. After all, it was Guruji who had to fast until death. The people were merely his supporters. There was also smoke in the air, and an expert nose could distinguish different varieties of narcotics.

The police were instructed to act leniently. The chief minister was aware that any dramatic action by the police would be milked by his opponents. This was the modus operandi that he was well aware of. Also, there was no point in catching people drinking in public. It was a matter of time before booze would be issued in rations.

Even though the movement was against the government, he was a part of, Deputy CM Banke attended the opening ceremony. "I will be attending the opening ceremony as a mark of respect for Guruji," he tweeted.

The opposition leaders wanted to milk the protest to the hilt, so they were constantly expressing their outrage at reporters on the ground and squabbling noisily during TV studio debates. The entire state was glued to the TV sets, and the TRP had gone through the roof, more so for the AAM channel, which had its cameras closest to Guruji—an exclusive privilege.

But the one who was basking in the glory with all the attention was Tanvi Mehra. In just a day, she became a household name and a celebrity. "Is she the dark horse in the CM's race?" Ananya Dutt, an influential political editor wrote, citing similarities with what had happened five years back. When Ananya Dutt wrote, people took note, and as a result, Tanvi's inbox was flooded with messages, many from people who, till yesterday, considered her a pariah.

All of a sudden, she was more powerful and famous than Soundarya Kapoor.

Success has many friends.

But this time, she would pay back with interest to all those who went after her.

After the *noch lenge* number, Gabru took a break while someone from his troop sang one of his songs. Gabru needed to refuel and headed to his vanity van, where he took out the packet tucked in his underwear. It was cocaine—his choice of drug. It was expensive, but then he was a rich man.

His last song had ten million hits on YouTube and was bought by a film producer making a movie on Naxals. Gabru had a farmhouse on the outskirts of V-AN where anyone from his village could come and stay for months. He was also a generous man and owed the generosity to the almighty who had made a matric fail into a superstar.

This was his fourth snort of the evening, and he was on a psychedelic slope. He heard the music dying, and now it was his turn. He was so eager to get to the stage that he didn't even wipe his nose.

Teri ma behen ek kar denge. He started again, and the crowds went ballistic.

Lovely and Fattu were sipping rum coke and watching the show from afar. They wore black suits, which Lovely had chosen as an action rig of Ghatak gang. It was inspired by the gangster movies he was so fond of. "Even if we get killed, it will be in style," Lovely had told Fattu in the tailor's shop.

Lovely checked his watch and looked at Fattu. The time had come. They gulped the remaining rum coke and took out an effigy from the wooden crate tucked in the bushes. Lovely held one bamboo leg and Fattu the other, and they started walking towards the stage.

Fattu also wore a portable loudspeaker on a shoulder sling and started yelling, "Siddheshwar Gupta *Haye Haye*." Such was the naked rage in his voice that soon, the crowds joined him, and at one point, *teri ma behen* was drowned by *haye haye*.

They were only ten feet away from the stage when, upon receiving an eye signal from Lovely, Fattu took out a kerosene bottle from his pocket and doused the effigy. Once satisfied that it was flammable, Lovely lighted a cigarette, then took a puff before torching.

Lovely raised the burning effigy of Siddheshwar Gupta, and

protestors threw stones at it. The passionate drunk crowd was dancing and making a deafening sound. Still, despite the noise and bluster, just like Arjun in Mahabharata, Lovely's eyes were on his aim—the diesel tank next to the power generator on the right side of the stage.

He remembered the love of his life, Tanvi Mehra, and threw the burning effigy towards the tank with full force. It only took seconds for the fire to spread to the stage. Guruji had been moved from the stage to his rest house fifteen minutes before.

Gabru was not so lucky. He could see his end coming.

He fearlessly jumped into the inferno.

Kishen

The cracks in the government over FLS were out in the open when Deputy CM Banke was spotted at Victoria Park. Though he tried to look agonised while explaining to the reporters the reason for his presence: 'Mark of respect to Guruji', 'To unite the citizens', etc.—it was evident that he was beaming from within.

His ambition to become the CM was well known. Five years back, he had been forced to yield space to the young and novice, but nonetheless popular and well-liked Siddheshwar Gupta. Reluctantly, he had agreed to become a deputy of someone who was way junior to him in politics and age. At that time, he was sanguine that he would get a shot at the top and had started working to destabilise the government from day one.

To his dismay, Siddheshwar kept surviving and getting stronger, and his own position kept weakening. Worse, he was caricatured as a comedian by Siddheshwar's gang. He hated Siddheshwar Gupta. But apart from him, he hated two others even more fervently.

One was Meenakshi Tandon, who considered him a village-born imbecile and treated him like one. He was delighted that she had ditched Gupta soon after making him sign a terrible decision. One should never give free liquor to people. It had to be given as a reward for something minor like attending rallies or major like committing murders.

The other one was Bhoomi Pracharak. If he had to pinpoint one person who had made him a joker in the eyes of the people, it was Bhoomi, who, at the direction of Siddheshwar Gupta, had run a concentrated campaign to tarnish his image. So, when Bhoomi had called him the other day, he was surprised.

They had met at his house, and it was an excellent opportunity for Banke to strangle his neck. But then Bhoomi told him about the background of FLS, how Meenakshi Tandon had hatched the multi-crore scam and left after taking bribes and that he was disillusioned with Siddheshwar Gupta and GKP. Banke would have still strangled his neck had he not come to the plan quickly.

Banke liked the plan. In fact, it was god-sent. As such, he was contemplating launching his own party or joining the opposition. However, if he could play his cards well in the next few days, he could get what he couldn't five years back. He just had to ensure he piggybacked on Guruji's agitation like Siddheshwar had done five years ago.

It was about to get dark, and it was time for him to sneak out of the park. After all, he had been there the whole day, and his Kishen was waiting for him at home. He instructed his PA to get the car ready at the VIP gate. However, as soon as he got up, he heard the announcement that Gabru would be performing next.

Banke changed his mind in a split second and decided to wait. He had seen Gabru's music videos and couldn't resist seeing him live. He sat back down and surreptitiously emptied the gutka packet into his mouth.

Fifteen minutes later, Banke was spellbound. The excitement in his loins reached a peak when Gabru removed his jacket. Unable to control himself, he ran towards the car, and his staff, security, and guard dogs followed.

When he reached his house, he found that the party had already started. His Kishen was seated on the throne, surrounded by singers and dancers gyrating on folk numbers. Banke almost ran and hugged him and sat next to him. Kishen passed his whisky glass to Banke. Having come from an anti-liquor event, Banke hesitated momentarily, but ignoring Kishen and resisting the temptation to enjoy single malt was impossible. He took a hungry gulp.

An hour later, drinks flowed, and at some point, Kishen started slithering to the beats of the music, offering currency notes to the dancers. An excited Banke yelled at Bhola, who was quietly watching the show from the far corner, to bring in a pile of cash from the almirah, and soon, the room was carpet-bombed with money.

At some point, Kishen removed his shirt, and Banke started caressing his body. It was still as tight as when they used to win local wrestling championships. In a swift movement, Banke took Kishen in his arms and kissed him, and then they both started dancing together.

Little did Banke know that his passion would cost him dearly.

Guilt

She sprang up from the bed, sweat-soaked and with a pounding heart. The images of Gabru engulfed in the fire were tormenting her. She had been with Guruji when the incident had occurred, and as soon as she heard the ear-deafening cries, she raced to the stage but froze when she saw him melting in the fire. By the time the firefighters arrived, his skin, tissues, and bones had turned into ashes.

She had never wanted something like that to happen. Her only instruction to him was to burn the effigy to grab headlines. It was also symbolic because the effigy of the then chief minister was burnt at the same venue five years back. She had given him a window when Guruji would not be on stage because he would not approve of an act like that. She should have known that he was not to be trusted.

She strained to look at the radium-lit dials of the wall clock. It was 2 am, and someone was incessantly ringing the doorbell. She saw through the peephole, and as expected, it was him. He was the last person she wanted to see, but then he was not the kind of person one should mess with. She rotated the lock lever and pressed the button.

He hurriedly embraced her and then forced a kiss on her lips, which made her flinch because she despised him, and he was reeking of liquor and cheap perfume.

"How was it?" He asked excitedly, expecting a pat on his back.

"He died."

"So that's good, right? The story is everywhere, and they are going to hang Siddheshwar Gupta. Right?" He asked again, this time more forcefully.

When Tanvi didn't reply, Lovely took her arm and dragged her in front of the TV. He switched it on to show her multiple feeds of midnight protests. A minibus was torched not far from where they were standing.

"Ghatak did this," Lovely said proudly.

Before Tanvi could react, there was breaking news.

Section 144 imposed.

"Ha-ha." Lovely gave out a deadly laugh. "This is the power of the Ghatak gang. We have brought the city to its knees."

He expected Tanvi to join him in cheering, but anger rose in him when he saw her worried face.

"What is wrong with you? I did everything for you," he said, tightening his grip on her wrist.

"Probably, we could have avoided a death and still caused the damage. You didn't have to ignite the fuel."

"Then you selected the wrong person to do the job because when Godfather strikes, he strikes with full vengeance and didn't that addict voluntarily jump into the fire?"

Tanvi felt a strange coldness in his voice, as if he could harm her in the next moment. She needed to urgently change tracks.

"You did good." She forced a cheer.

Lovely's mood changed instantaneously, and he loosened his grip. This time, he kissed her tenderly and led her to the bedroom.

Lovely had left an hour back, but she still couldn't sleep. She was tossing and turning, reasoning with herself. She was in this to win. Guilt would only weaken her, and it was not worth crying for a cocaine addict who had committed suicide.

The doctor monitoring Guruji's condition had warned her last evening that he should stop fasting. She couldn't let that happen, could she? More so when she was so close to victory. Tomorrow,

GCI stock would reach the same level as before the announcement of FLS, and it would be a matter of time before all this was over. Guruji needed to keep his fast till then.

At some point, she drifted off to sleep—free of any worry or guilt.

Silver Lining

His worst nightmare had come true. His mentor was fasting against him. Guruji looked old and feeble; forget fasting. Should he even be out in the cold? He had sent a request to meet him. It was declined with a caveat that only the withdrawal of FLS could make it possible. That was the problem with Guruji's approach to life.

He was unbending and always put his ideals over everything else. That was also the reason for their fallout five years back. He had asked him to refrain from forming a political party, knowing well that if they didn't capitalise on public sentiment, all the effort would go down the drain.

Also, serving people couldn't be done just out of altruistic desire. Self-interest and personal ambitions were also driving factors. The results were decent. He brought in his unique model of governance. FEWS benefited lakhs of citizens, and now FLS would bring much-needed happiness.

Gabru's death sent shock waves, and there were riots last night. He had expected FLS to be controversial, but had not imagined that the reactions would be so violent. That's why Meenakshi had left after making her money. He grudgingly admired her cunning. Even though it was evident that she had backstabbed him and made a fool out of him, a part of his mind still wanted to give her the benefit of doubt.

It was foolishness, but isn't love the same?

His approval ratings, which had bumped up on the day of the introduction of FLS, were tapering off. Still, if he could control the slide, he would have a fair shot at winning. The problem was that the continuation of Guruji's fast could hamper all his plans. And then who was this Tanvi Mehra? He had got a dossier on her.

Nothing extraordinary, except for that she ran some sort of club with Soundarya Kapoor. But nothing was extraordinary about him also when he ran for the elections five years back. The only thing of interest was that she recently had had a bitter fallout with Soundarya Kapoor.

He was furious when he was informed that Banke Singh was at Victoria Park. How could his deputy, a member of his cabinet, take part in an agitation against his own government of which he was a part? Banke had to be taught a lesson.

Such was the hatred between the brothers that Bhola needed no convincing. After clicking the pictures of Banke dancing and making love, he came straight to the CM secretariat, where a team of IT experts worked together to put out a tweet from Banke's own account at midnight. The midnight tweet had Banke holding a whisky glass and kissing his boyfriend. It was captioned: "Just back from *Andolan*—Work Hard, Party Harder." #forFLS #supportFLS.

The tweet went viral by sunrise, and as expected, he received Banke's resignation. Banke followed it with a press release that his account had been hacked and fake photos were uploaded. He also directly alleged that CM Siddheshwar and large corporates were behind the conspiracy as he was protesting against FLS. He said he would keep supporting the agitation and sit beside Guruji and fast.

Siddheshwar read the statement and smiled. Despite what that joker had written, one thing was clear from the picture. Liquor did bring happiness. He had never seen Banke so calm, so much in love, and so humane. This itself was the most authentic feedback on FLS.

There were also news reports on how people were drunk at the rally and how much cocaine Gabru had consumed before jumping into the fire. FLS would cure binge drinking and drug addiction by providing calibrated doses of nectar, so that a person only experienced a decent high with no side effects and hangover.

As he reread Banke's resignation letter, he realised there were a few silver linings even on this gloomy day.

Cursed Winner

The race between them had been over a long time ago, and she had won that race. The fear that her gold medal could be taken away was traumatic. When she saw Tanvi's photos on the front pages that morning, she felt that fear. Tanvi leading the protest against FLS was the biggest shock of her life.

How did she get the information in advance which only a few were aware of? The puzzle was solved when she heard Bhoomi Pracharak speak against FLS while interviewing Tanvi. Both her enemies had joined hands and now they were going after her only lease of life.

But it was not only that. Tanvi had become the flavour of the season overnight. Ananya Dutt extolled her virtues in her popular editorial, "After a long time in my career as a political journalist, I have seen a woman with a steely resolve that reminds me of an ex-PM. Her height and sharp features give her a distinctive and striking appearance. Her intelligence, wit and ability to think on her feet make her a force to reckon with. The way she handled the first day of the movement is admirable."

After reading it, Soundarya felt that the gold medal she had adorned for years was melting into a dark sludge, and once again, she was back into the race, and unless she took urgent actions, she could come out as a loser this time.

Tanvi was unpredictable; she always had been, as far as she could remember, which made her so dangerous. A chameleon who could smooth talk her way through any situation. She was the most popular girl in school and college, and her numerous admirers used to eat from her hands.

Soundarya, on the other hand, was a pimple-infested plain Jane in staid kurta pyjamas. No one gave her a second glance. Then, one day, she had to drop out of college, and slowly, everyone forgot about her, not that anyone had cared to begin with. Her fate changed when she got married to Kiku Kapoor. Everything changed overnight, including her epidermis and iris, transforming her into a green-eyed beauty with translucent skin.

They say the winner takes it all, and she had emerged as a winner. Those who were even unwilling to recognise her existence started worshipping her. Tanvi Mehra was one of them, though Soundarya kept her distance from her for the first fifteen years after she moved to Victoria. Only in the last five years did she let her in her life because she had gone miles ahead of her and realised that the real fun of winning was to keep the loser in the vicinity.

That was a mistake for which she was paying the price now.

The situation was grim, and she had asked Brown to give funds to organise a counter-protest. After all, once Tipsy World Wine (TWW) bought out GCI, TWW would be the ultimate beneficiary of FLS. The problem was that Brown was dilly-dallying. He was a shrewd bastard who wanted GCI to put the money. Soundarya would have, but the problem was that the cash flow was tight. In fact, GCI had taken on more debt to increase production to fulfil the massive demand of FLS.

Another stone in her shoe was her mother-in-law. She was incessantly sending her threatening and hurtful messages. She could read between the lines and imagine her rage. She gave that to her; no grief was as painful as the loss of a son, but then, after a point, it became too much to take.

Sumitra Kapoor was alleging that she had killed Kiku. It was partly true. Soundarya had replaced his beta-blocker, which he took daily for lowering heartbeat, with steroids a couple of days before his death. She had no alternative because for FLS to become a law, GCI had to marry TWW. But then he actually died because of exertion for which, if anyone was to be blamed, was his personal trainer.

Thankfully, Sumitra Kapoor was under house arrest under the supervision of a psychiatrist and his team of nurses. On Soundarya's directives, she was kept under heavy sedatives, but even then, she was sending these messages. She had asked the nurse in attendance to confiscate her phone, but that turned out to be a tough act.

Sumitra started banging her head on the wall in protest, and the scared nurse returned the phone. She would have to stop her, or else soon, everyone would start suspecting Kiku's death was unnatural. Still thinking, she opened M&S. There was a notification:

Toni left.

She was still in shock when another message beeped. It was from Jo.

'Sorry, hon, I will have to cancel the party. Not well. Loosies.'

Another surprise! Was all this a coincidence, or had the tide turned? She had to do something fast.

Hit it where it hurts the most

"Gabru's death is a minor setback in an otherwise great start, but it is a setback." Bhoomi nudged his horn-rimmed glasses up the bridge of his nose. His pepper-salt hair was set so neatly that Tanvi suspected that he wore a wig. Tanvi was in a beige saree and a full-sleeved blouse. "Female politicians must not display an ounce of skin," she was advised by the man sitting in front of her. It was depressing that she would have to maintain a façade of simplicity and prudishness for the rest of her life if her career as a politician took off.

On hearing the soft crack of the door behind, she turned her neck and saw his secretary carrying a bottle of wine. Her red dress clung to every curve of her body as she poured the crimson liquid into the crystal glasses on the round dining table at the far end of his massive office, adorned with a dozen trophies. There were also framed pictures of him with celebrities, but the one thing which confirmed that he was a narcissist was his portrait in which he held a globe in his hands.

The secretary left soon after, and Bhoomi stood, picked up the glasses from the table, and passed one to Tanvi. He was wearing a navy-blue suit and a red tie. Though he was a fit man, there was something feminine about the way he walked.

"I need one of these before going live," he said, as if trying to justify.

Tanvi stirred her glass and smelt. It was fantastic, and it was what her aching bones needed. The second day of the movement was unremarkable compared to the first, which was not such a bad thing.

Earlier, Toni had called her to tell that he had left M&S. He also expressed his undying loyalty to her and urged her to create a new group and even suggested the name M&S (O), O for Original.

"You have much more class and taste than Soundarya Kapoor. She thinks people don't know where she comes from. You just say yes, and I will throw the biggest party this city has ever seen." He also bragged how he had threatened Jo not to throw the M&S party on Saturday.

This was good news. Toni leaving the group and Jo cancelling the party were good signs, which would have given Soundarya jitters.

Just wait, bitch. I have many more aces up my sleeve.

Her phone rang. It was Lovely. She disconnected and put her phone in silent mode.

"But what do you think about Banke sharing the stage with Guruji now? He is even fasting," she asked.

"Let's wait and watch. If we have to sacrifice him, we will do it when it benefits us the most," Bhoomi said and refilled his glass to the brim.

So, it was not just a glass for him before he annihilated people in his popular 9 pm debate, Tanvi thought.

"Ananya Dutt has asked me to give her an interview."

Bhoomi's face tightened.

"You can't do that. You are exclusive to me, and don't think you can become the next CM because she said so. Your destiny is in my control."

The mask was off.

Tanvi resisted the temptation to throw the wine on his face. It was difficult to deal with a narcissist, but it was not impossible if you knew which buttons to push.

She stood, walked up to him, and gave him a semi-hug, her fingers brushing his. "I am your prodigy."

Bhoomi gave a victorious grin and poured more wine.

They did their cheers again and drank till the production assistant rushed into the room and said, "30 seconds to go."

Bhoomi looked at Tanvi with conceit and then polished off the glass in one go. The 9 pm debate started a minute later:

"FLS is a rotten scheme. It will corrode the frame of society. In the garb of spreading happiness, they will ruin the future of present and future generations. To hell with this scheme."

Tanvi watched him thunder on the screen. She was still in his office.

GKP supporters on the debate were confused. Wasn't Bhoomi their man? The opposition sympathisers were equally confused. A social activist asked him if his loyalties had shifted.

"It has nothing to do with loyalty. One has to have a moral compass, and who will benefit from this; the GCI, the corrupt company that was cooking its books for a long time before an activist stock firm went after it. We cannot let Soundarya Kapoor win because she represents the sins in our society."

His last sentence was music to Tanvi's ears. She savoured the last of the wine and decided to leave. Tomorrow was going to be a long day.

She left Bhoomi's office and passed through the receptionist's desk, who gave her a furtive glance—*perks of being famous.*

She came out of the building and lit a cigarette. Her second of the day. She had suppressed her urge all day because cameras followed her wherever she went. Anyway, it was good. Cigarette, after a gap, gave real pleasure. The parking lot was almost deserted, and there was an eerie silence. Suddenly, she longed for bed.

Then she remembered that Ashok had moved out last night. Though it was good that he had realised their paths were different, she still felt a tinge of sadness. He had been a loyal companion to her for all these years. But now, the time had come to part ways, and she was relieved that Ashok had left without any emotional drama. She was incapable of dealing with emotions. She made a mental note to call the lawyer; an amicable divorce was the best way forward.

Someone else may come up. Right now, her career was a priority. She stubbed the cigarette and started walking towards her car. She loved it—a navy-blue Beamer, the top model of the category. She took out the key from her bag. The key was encased in soft brown leather, and she loved caressing it.

She was smiling when she pressed the button.

They say one sees their whole life pass by when one is dying.

In her case, it was only Soundarya Kapoor.

Pompous Men

"Why did you kill her? Are you insane? You have jeopardised everything," Robert Brown hollered on the phone. Soundarya disconnected without uttering a word and removed the driver from her golf bag. She wanted to concentrate on the game, but the phone call made her mind wander to the first time she had played a round of golf with her father-in-law and two other pompous men. When it was her turn, she had chosen the driver.

One pompous man had told her mockingly to play with an iron instead—a safer option. Soundarya had disregarded the unsolicited advice and swung the driver, but duffed the shot. The snooty men didn't try to suppress their laughter. She had to tee off again, and practicality meant using an iron club the second time.

Instead, she again took the driver and hit a shot 50 yards ahead of the men. Gulab Chand's chest had swelled with pride, but the other two egoists sulked the remaining round.

Robert Brown should know whom he was dealing with. He was an educated Westerner, but that made him no less patriarchal. Men like him believed, no matter what, a woman could be forced into submission. In contrast, there were men like Gulab Chand who felt proud when women succeeded—unfortunately, such men were in short supply.

After a straight drive to the fairway, she chipped the ball next to the pin, putted it, and ended up with a birdie. Walking towards the second hole, anger rose in her, and she texted Robert Brown—*Fuck you, the deal is off!*

The late-night incident in front of the AAM office was all over the news. The opposition was accusing Siddheshwar Gupta of murder. The images of the BMW charred to pieces, its body dented and twisted, and glass and metal scattered all around were viral. Since the incident had occurred in front of the AAM office, there was live coverage of flames, smoke, and sirens, and Tanvi Mehra on the stretcher.

Tanvi's popularity was rising by the hour. There were yagnas happening in many parts of the city for her well-being. Even Guruji came out with the statement, "Tanvi Mehra is a faithful worker. I pray for her long life."

What if she dies? Won't she become a martyr?

The thought disturbed Soundarya so much that she hit the next shot into the water. But she soon recovered when she remembered Rameshwaram's assurance, "It would be fire, not a blast."

He was watching her and would have defused the bomb if she was less than fifty feet from the car. He had also siphoned off the petrol beforehand so that the explosion was not uncontrolled. All the planning was his. What a talented man he was; she admired him.

He could have been in NASA, but instead, he preferred to be her servant—the epitome of loyalty, people who pay back their entire life. He had made the IED in his quarter using fertilisers and some wires. He had also spoofed the sophisticated BMW lock—an ingenious man indeed.

Robert Brown called back, but she disconnected at the first ring. Let him sweat.

There were only two types of people who were not afraid of consequences—very rich or very poor, and she had been on both sides. Let TWW revoke its offer. FLS was a law, and GCI would survive, but she was sure that greedy bastard would return to her with a begging bowl.

The ninth hole of VGC was called the peacock hole. A par three next to the clubhouse. Soundarya's first shot landed two feet from the hole. She finished with a birdie. Everyone sitting in the club clapped, and she basked in adulation.

Once in the ladies' room, she got rid of her sweaty clothes and stood under the shower for a long time, reminiscing about her golf rounds with Gulab Chand. She missed him. She changed into a long white cotton dress, red woollen jacket and matching flip-flops and walked to the adjoining bar named Nineteenth Hole.

She always liked to drink beer after golf, just like her father-in-law. The first sip was amazing. She was sitting on a table at the far corner of the bar with her back towards the long end of the hall. She wanted to avoid attention and drink in solitude. Midway through the second pint, she saw the news flash on the TV screen on the opposite wall—'Tanvi Mehra's condition is stable'.

She was relieved. She didn't want her to die like that because it would have been too easy. She asked for a strong LIT.

It was time for serious drinking.

It was war.

Gulaabo

There are many theories about how 'rum' originated. There is a mention even in Sanskrit about a drink produced by fermentation and distillation of sugarcane juice used as a medicine prescribed by doctors. The history tells that the rum may have originated in many countries and regions, including a Spanish warship. However, it is widely believed that rum actually took off once it reached the Caribbean and became a drink of choice at parties for the wealthy.

Gulab Chand Kapoor was already a wealthy farmer before he started GCI. The idea came up during a trip to Barbados, and his distilling plant was up and running in six months. He had to select a name for his dark rum. He got a hint when he noticed that whenever people drank his rum, their cheeks turned pink with joy, and therefore, he decided to call it Gulaabo.

He opened many factories throughout the country, but his first was at Victoria, which was regarded as its flagship factory. It was a matter of pride for Kapoors that a visit to their factory was on the itinerary of tourists visiting the city.

Back then, marketing was an enormous challenge. The media's reach was minimal. Also, the way it is produced, rum is cheaper than whisky or wine. Therefore, the target was the mass market that could afford Gulaabo, and Gulab Chand ran the most ingenious marketing campaign. Two types of celebrities were popular—film stars and cricketers.

Gulab Chand made friends with both kinds, hosted parties, attended matches and premiers, and ensured that a bottle of Gulaabo was in every picture frame. Many movies in the '70s and '80s had the hero drinking Gulaabo after a heartbreak or before breaking the bones of the villain. If nothing else, a vamp would dance around with a bottle of Gulaabo. Similarly, if his cricketer friend made a century or took wickets, he would give an interview in a Gulaabo t-shirt. Soon, Gulaabo became the drink of choice for the population.

His other marketing genius was that even though it was cheap, he made Gulaabo exclusive. He always ensured that the supply was less than the demand, so much so that people considered it good luck if they could get Gulaabo from a wine shop. After the success of Gulaabo, GCI ventured into soaps, shampoos and even biscuits. Still, nothing succeeded as much, and GCI and Gulaabo became synonymous.

At the turn of the century, restrictions were lifted, and many international players entered the arena. They had well-recognised brands in their kitty and tons of marketing dollars. Slowly, Gulaabo sales started dwindling. Kiku's mismanagement was another reason for the decline. Unlike his father, he neither had the talent nor the drive.

But Gulaabo was still loved.

FLS was an opportunity for Gulaabo to get to where it deserved to be.

Inferno

They were a bottle down when Fattu took out the chit. He expertly sprinkled the powder on the Metro card, made a line, and took a deep snort. He then tapped Lovely's shoulder and offered. Lovely saw the powder and caught Fattu's collar, "*Behenchod,* what are you doing?"

"Bhai, you also do it. It will help us," Fattu stammered.

Instead, a livid Lovely gave him a tight slap on the face, and the card flew away. One more on the back of his head, and Fattu was in tears. Lovely held his head in a vice-like grip and brought his face close to his own till their noses were touching, and blurted out the lines which his Godfather Vito Corleone had spoken with such élan, "I will never allow drugs in this city, I am okay with everything else; smuggling, betting and even prostitution, but drugs are something which will destroy the future generations of this fine city."

Fattu sheepishly took out two more packets from his underwear and emptied the contents into the sewer his father would clean the next day. Then he took an oath, "*Ma kasam,* never again."

Lovely's face softened, and he passed a fresh drink to Fattu. "Here, let's drink one more before we get on with it."

They gulped their drinks and then made last-minute preparations. Their kit bags contained fifty gelatine sticks each and ammonium nitrate. For this job, they chucked the suits and wore overalls instead.

They had already kidnapped the head guard earlier in the day and planted their man in his place. Their tempo had six oak barrels to be delivered to the GCI factory. It was past midnight, and they slowly drove to their destination, hoping there was no police checkpoint en route. When they reached the factory gate, they were momentarily stopped but were soon waved off by their own man.

They had painstakingly gone through the factory layout and had planned to plant the bombs at the third building from the gate, which housed the main distilling plant. They had reckoned that a blast there would cause the maximum damage. They parked their tempo outside the plant and carried an oak barrel inside the plant.

A few workers inside were moving up and down, and the supervisor was sleeping on his desk. No one paid attention to them as the factory kept getting barrel supplies all day to meet the FLS demand. In any case, they were ready if someone would have tried to stop them.

The gelatine had to be placed in the most combustible places, and they knew the exact locations. They got to work and stuck the ammunition below every boiler, evaporator, and tank in the next fifteen minutes. Once they had finished, they kept the remaining oak barrels on the shop floor. They woke up the supervisor to get the delivery challan signed.

Once they were out of the main gate, they took out the detonator.

An earth-shattering blast was followed by fire and dense smoke. About twenty fire tenders and five ambulances raced towards the GCI factory, their sirens blaring. Soon, the air was thick with the acrid smell of burning chemicals and ash.

Fifteen workers died.

Gulab Chand's pride, his first factory, was reduced to a pile of debris.

Facial Recognition System

A person will keep committing sins if there are no consequences, but once he or she is aware of both good and bad, he will make informed choices. This principle governed the workings of the world.

You steal, you go to jail.

You kill, you go to gallows.

You don't support FLS, you will not be given liquor.

That morning, a decree was signed by Siddheshwar Gupta that anyone not in support of FLS would be debarred from consuming liquor and would be excluded from FLS for one year. People were confused because FLS was voluntary, and 'milk in lieu of liquor' was part of FLS. The clarity emerged once they read the fine print of the order. The order was specifically for those taking part in the protests at Victoria Park.

It said that the Facial Recognition System (FRS) had been installed at each entry point of Victoria Park. The faces of those attending the *andolan* would be matched with their Aadhar numbers, and they would receive the notification of the liquor ban on their registered mobile numbers.

The first few hundred who reached the park that morning got the SMS after fifteen minutes. The word spread rapidly, and vehicles approaching Victoria Park took a U-turn. By noon, Victoria Park was almost deserted. Even members of the *bhajan* group, which was being paid to perform, were missing.

Since the band was not complete, they started playing recorded music. The hawkers were worst affected and incurred heavy losses as they had stocked perishable food in anticipation of strong demand.

"This is masterstroke, Sir," Bhola complimented his boss. Since the day he had proved his loyalty, they had become close. They say that blood is thicker than water, but it is also true that sibling rivalry can make people kill. In one stroke, Bhola had avenged all the humiliation he had suffered at the hands of Banke.

They were watching the deserted VC Park on the TV. Guruji had not come onto the stage, and there was a statement that his health condition had deteriorated. *That was wise,* Siddheshwar thought, because getting Guruji in front of a meagre crowd would only lower his heft and position. He was surprised that none of the opposition leaders had also come. This proved that to whatever extent they went after FLS, nobody wanted the risk of a personal ban.

He had taken the decision at midnight after the fire in the GCI factory. He wanted protestors to know the price, and also, it was essential to stop Guruji somehow. He had first-hand experience of how each hour of his fast consolidated public support behind him. He would not resort to *lathi charge* or filling up jails. That would boomerang. Instead, he would just exclude those people from FLS. Isn't that what they wanted in the first place and were protesting for?

His IT minister had come up with a suggestion for how to do it. Overnight, FRS was installed using emergency purchasing power and was already giving results.

Some more breaking news, and all of a sudden, there was a live feed from the courts where two lawyers were arguing, "How can there be a rule like that? If one protests against FLS, that does not mean that person cannot or doesn't like to drink with his hard-earned money; how can you deny him?"

The other lawyer spoke in between, "So, the problem is that you want to deny the poor a dose of happiness."

Siddheshwar Gupta knew that the court would eventually quash the rule, but it would buy him some time, which is exactly what he needed. He had directed his law minister to delay everything as much as possible. If required, the roads leading to the court building could be dug up, or electricity and water connections could be snapped.

The protest had to stop at any cost.

He called Police Commissioner Nand Kishore to find out if there were any leads on the fire in the GCI factory. Like always, Nand Kishore assured him they were close to a breakthrough. The CM warned him to catch the culprits in the next 24 hours, or he could pack his bags and shift to Timbak Tu.

"I want you to conduct a press conference within 24 hours in which you would give details of the culprits behind the blast," he said.

If it came out that the protestors were behind the factory burning, it would be good press. He called Soundarya Kapoor again. No answer. Where the hell was she?

Do Not Disturb

She had shifted to Diplomat after Kiku's death. There was no way she could stay with her mother-in-law at Kapoor villa. Last night, she had barely managed to stagger back to her suite. Too many LITs. Before crashing, she had put 'Do Not Disturb' outside her room and switched off her mobile.

She opened her eyes to the knocks on the door and tried to orient herself. Someone was vigorously knocking on the door. She cursed and slept again, but not for too long. The soft knocks soon gave way to loud thuds, and she was suddenly wide awake. She opened the door. The messenger looked apologetic but said rather firmly, "The CM wants to urgently speak to you."

"What's the time?"

"Half-past twelve."

Somehow, Soundarya knew something terrible had happened, but at the same time, she felt relaxed and refreshed. She had needed a good night's sleep, and LITs had done the trick. She brought her phone out of airplane mode and immediately noticed the flood of notifications. She opened the one from her secretary. *I am so sorry, ma'am, I am at the factory.*

She didn't have to read all the sympathetic messages to figure out what had happened. It was breaking news.

GCI Victoria factory burnt to ashes.

She suddenly remembered her father-in-law telling her during a round of the factory, "Of all the things I have done, I am most proud of this factory. My blood and sweat have gone into building this."

It was indeed special, unlike the tasteless brick-and-mortar factory they built nowadays. It had a facade in brick stone, marble cladding on the walls and airy workspaces. It was in the commercial district of Victoria, surrounded by 5-star hotels, fine restaurants and high-street malls and sat on super expensive land.

Is it such bad news? Soundarya thought after the initial shock weaned off. She couldn't sell the factory because it would mean a betrayal of her father-in-law's feelings, but now there was no factory. She knew it was Tanvi's strike, a return of favour, after what she did to her car. She would strike back, but first, she needed to do a few important things. She called Siddheshwar Gupta.

"Where the hell are you?" The CM asked in a panic-filled voice.

"I have been busy. I know you are concerned about the factory, but the reality is that it is only a quarter of our production capacity. You need not worry; it will not affect the roll-out of FLS," she assured him.

"If you say so." Siddheshwar sounded unsure.

"Now, you can arrest Tanvi Mehra," Soundarya asked.

"How can we? She is in hospital," he replied in an incredulous voice.

"You know, and I know, and everyone knows how she did it."

"Nand Kishore is looking into it; I have asked him to make an arrest in twenty-four hours. I basically called you to express my sympathies."

"My people died, and whosoever is responsible for the death of my people will repay with interest." She thanked him and disconnected the phone.

She then called up Robert Brown.

"We will be using one of your production facilities." It was more of an order than a request.

Robert Brown agreed in an instant. In any case, Gulaabo would be his soon and why not start taking control now.

She read about FRS and finally smiled.

Sweet Revenge

Tanvi opened her eyes and found him sitting on the chair beside her bed. His eyes were closed, his head tilted to one side, and his chest was heaving up and down like that of a tired soul getting much-needed rest. At that moment, he looked more like an angel than a gangster.

She knew he was there to get his reward for what he had done last night. Though she would feign ignorance in front of him, she had been closely monitoring the events through the night. She got the confirmation that everything was going according to plan when she heard the fire brigade sirens. GCI factory was not very far from where she was.

It was sweet revenge.

But still, there was a long way to go before she put the final nail in her coffin.

The FRS brought in by the CM could ruin everything. The matter was in the court, but the more it lingered on, the more the chances that the movement would die down. She needed to quickly come up with a Plan B. As she stirred in her bed, Lovely woke up with a start.

Ho gaya, he said and gave a satisfied look.

She actually wanted to tell him to fuck off. His visiting her in the hospital was dangerous. She was sure that the police would be after him soon and that it would not be too difficult to connect the dots. Still, for now, she had to make sure that Lovely basked in the glory.

"My hero, I am so proud of you," she said in a sleepy, sweet voice.

"Perfect *tha, rakh rakh ho gaya* (It was perfect. It turned into ashes.)," His voice quivered with pride.

"Did anyone see you?"

"No, no, our faces were covered."

"Great," Tanvi replied, knowing very well that he would have left a dozen clues.

"Are you fine now?" He asked with concern.

"Yes, I am."

"Ok, let's get out of here. I have a car."

No way was she going to go with him.

"I will stay for one more night as per doctor's advice; why take chances?" She reasoned.

Lovely's face fell flat, but then he quickly reconciled. "Yes, you are right, one more night is a good idea. As such, I am busy tonight. Ghatak has got a new contract."

The way he said it made Tanvi feel that she was now a gangster's wife.

She will have to do something about him.

"I will come back tomorrow, same time, and we will go out and celebrate."

"Yes, we will," she said and forced a smile.

"I still have to catch the person who burnt your car," he said before finally leaving the room.

As soon as he was gone, Tanvi called up Bhoomi, "The movement will die if we don't do anything fast."

"Are you aware of the fire at GCI?"

"Yes, I came to know; will it affect?"

"Don't think so. They are saying that this particular factory only produced twenty-five per cent. I have also heard that GCI is shifting some production to TWW. She will probably capitalise on this. The piece of land is already on the market."

This struck Tanvi. She had not thought of it. The land was in a prime location and would fetch her good money. However, her first worry was the movement.

"I have thought about it. We will shift the venue to Azaad Maidan, where no camera *shamera* would work. Tomorrow, Guruji will lead a route march from Victoria Park to Azaad Maidan. Also, we will need to get people from neighbouring states so that we have the largest crowd ever seen."

"It will cost a lot."

"Tell your friends to shell out because if they don't, their coffers will eventually dry."

"I will try," Bhoomi replied non-committedly.

Tanvi walked to the balcony adjoining her VIP room and lit a cigarette. "It's up to them. It doesn't make a difference to me."

"I will try my best."

"That's like it."

After stubbing out the cigarette and washing her face, she connected with Guruji.

"Guruji, I am fine by the grace of God and yours."

"Tanvi *beta,* I am so relieved."

"Guruji, I am planning to shift the venue. Let's go to Azaad Maidan, where they cannot stop people."

"After what they did to you, I am more determined than ever."

Tanvi was excited that Guruji had readily accepted her plan.

Gold Room

"Which M&S?"

The question stumped the Dubeys.

"The M&S party?"

"Sir, there are two M&S parties happening tonight, one in Gold and the other in Silver," the concierge replied.

"The one which Soundarya Kapoor is hosting."

"That one is Silver."

"Who is hosting the other one?"

"Tanvi Mehra."

Dubeys were confused as well as stunned. This was the *dharam sankat* they were trying to avoid, though they would have gone to 'Silver' a week back without a second thought. But now that Tanvi Mehra's stock was rising rapidly, they had to be careful. The husband and wife got into a huddle and finally decided they should split. Mrs Dubey would go to Gold, and Mr Dubey would go to Silver.

The two banquets were next to each other, though, as the name suggested, Gold was superior to Silver with better furnishings, a nicer bar, and was larger. It was surprising to most that the party by Tanvi was in Gold and Soundarya in Silver. There was a flurry of calls and gossip the whole day amongst the members of M&S about how that was possible. The only plausible explanation was that Toni was now in Tanvi's camp, and no one could burn money as quickly as Toni. He would have made an insane bid to secure Gold.

Tanvi got a hero's welcome when she entered the party. She was still wearing the same beige saree she had worn the day of the accident. Except for the carbon flakes that had clung to her face and saree, she had come out unscathed from the explosion. Probably, the shock of seeing her car burn had made her faint.

Overall, it was a lucky save, but one she knew was well-planned. Soundarya Kapoor could have killed her if she wanted to. She didn't do it because this would have been a shallow victory for her. She would eventually like to kill her, but not before inflicting pain.

I would also do the same to her. Let's see who gets there first.

Attending the party that night was something she could have avoided, but Toni was vehement. Also, to have a party of breakaway M&S group was a sort of mini victory. She quickly scanned the room—there were about thirty there, so that meant around seventy were in the Silver room.

Tanvi quickly scanned the crowd—Malhotras, Shaina, Bunty Walia, Oberois—that was a surprise. A server offered champagne, but Tanvi declined. No way was she going to drink in public. She was sure many photographers were planted there just to catch her drinking the bubbly.

Instead, she asked for a cup of tea. It was the safest option, as allegations could be levelled that the juice she was drinking had liquor in it. Toni protested, but she cajoled him. "We can always drink later."

She went ahead and met everyone, thanking them for being there.

Nimish Malhotra was worried. "Are you really supporting prohibition?"

"Not actually; my protest is against free liquor, which will convert non-drinkers to drinkers."

"So basically, you are going after Soundarya and her GCI." Bunty Walia laughed, but Tanvi let it pass.

"Oh, nothing is going to happen to Victorians. Our life will remain unaffected," Shaina, a serial divorcee of wealthy men, gloated.

M&S parties were about booze, dancing and flirting, but they were also about photographs. For many, the next day's high of seeing themselves on page 3 and Facebook or Instagram was much more appealing than the party itself. So, there were cameramen present who would use the most advanced filters to lift the sagging skins, change the colour tones, chisel features, widen eyes and shrink bodies to give them an haute appearance.

Also, personal phones, such as iPhone Pro with artificial intelligence, transformed their owner's picture based on what they liked on Instagram. For the next fifteen minutes or so, everyone clicked pictures with rising star Tanvi Mehra, and those pictures were instantaneously uploaded on social media.

"I asked Moni to attend her party, to keep an eye on things," Toni told her after everyone was done taking pictures with her. Tanvi was not sure if that was the case. Moni hated her. But then, one way, it was better. She needed Toni's undivided support.

Suddenly, the lights dimmed, and the music changed to fast dance numbers.

***

When she was informed that the Gold room was taken, Soundarya had thrown a fit. "How can you do that?" She had shouted.

"Ma'am, the booking was confirmed around an hour back."

"Who booked it?"

"Toni Singh."

She understood the game. There was a domino effect after Toni left. Malhotras, Oberois and even Shaina, whom she had considered close to her, also left M&S.

She would not let anyone join back, even if they begged.

It was difficult to change the venue at the last moment. She had already sent out the invites. Then, an idea struck her, and she changed the theme of her party and made it an arty evening—paintings and ghazals. She called up an art gallery and asked them to send their paintings. She also prepared a response if someone questioned why the party was at Silver and not Gold. "Cosy evenings with intellectuals require understated elegance. Also, the acoustics are better in Silver."

After half an hour of the usual meet and greet, Soundarya felt that her party was dragging. Her guests had not even thrown a cursory glance at the paintings and did not at all acknowledge the efforts of Ghazab Ali, a clone of Ghulam Ali, as he sang in a dull and lifeless voice.

Sunil Arora was restless. Here, he was made to listen to sad ghazals, whereas people were dancing to fast numbers in the next room. He told his wife he was going to the washroom; instead, he went to the Gold room next door and left M&S in transit.

Vigs were also not too happy. It was their anniversary, and the ghazals by Ghazab Ali had made the atmosphere so gloomy that they feared they might end up divorcing each other by the end of the evening. So, they drank more. At some point, the music coming from the Gold room became so loud that the ghazal hum was suppressed entirely. Ghazab Ali stopped singing. He might be a clone, but he had an ego.

Soundarya was livid. She summoned the manager, but when he didn't come even after a long wait, she asked Dubey to go to Gold and get the music down. Dubey dilly-dallied at first, but when Soundarya hissed, he had nowhere to hide. He kept his glass down and left the Silver room with drooping shoulders. He didn't want to do the task, but was stuck. Soundarya's eagle eyes were following him.

He cautiously cracked open the Gold room door and saw the scenes inside. Everyone was dancing fervently to the beats of the music. Dubey wanted to leave and go home, but was worried about the repercussions. Also, Mrs Dubey was at that party, and strangely, she seemed to be enjoying herself dancing with Sunil Arora.

Jealousy struck Dubey. He was going to get the music stopped and take Mrs Dubey home. This was no way to behave. He quietly entered the hall and asked the passing server to request the DJ to lower the music. The server was half drunk and was enjoying the *tamasha*, so he ignored him. Why spoil the fun for an oldie?

Dubey then mustered courage and walked up to the DJ console. The DJ was a famous coke junkie who ignored Dubey's gestures. Finally, Dubey had to shake his shoulders to get attention. Irritated, the DJ removed his headphones and responded roughly, "What? Not taking requests."

"I am not here for a request; I want you to lower the volume."

Before DJ Wakil could answer, Dubey felt a hand on his shoulder. He turned back. It was a very drunk Toni.

"Hi, Toni ji, how are you?" Dubey greeted meekly.

"What do you want?" Toni growled.

Dubey knew it was best to keep quiet and leave, but just then, his eyes fell on Mrs Dubey, who was now doing a close dance with Sunil Arora. He could see his hand on her back slowly shifting lower. It had to be stopped before the disaster happened.

"Lower the bloody volume." His anger towards his wife resonated in his voice.

Instead of replying, Toni caught his collar. "*Behenchod,* who allowed you to come inside?" He then dragged Dubey outside the party and started slapping him in full view. A crowd congregated quickly to watch Dubey getting thrashed.

Dubey would have died had the hotel security not untangled them. Toni and Dubey were taken to their cars under security. Everyone left soon except for the two founders of M&S. They were both staring at each other with hate. However, if one would have noticed carefully, there was also a hint of a smile on their faces.

Azaad Maidan

Azaad Maidan came into existence a decade ago. Though the population of Azaad Nagar was ten times the population of Victoria, the number of parks in Victoria were ten times more. But then, no one cared.

The people of Azaad Nagar were so used to living in stifling surroundings characterised by overflowing sewers, leaking urinals, open defecation, effluents pouring out of illegal factories and diesel fumes from run-down vehicles that they had developed immunity to the ill effects of pollution. They comfortably lived with lungs full of tar and stomachs full of ulcers. On the contrary, a glass of clean water or a breath of fresh air made them sick.

So, no one cared till one day, the government decided to give them a park six months before the elections. Elaborate plans were made, and an architect from Singapore was hired. But then, it was not so easy. The first problem was to find a space. So high was its population density that AN didn't have an inch to spare.

But then, a wily official came up with a suggestion to convert the infamous Bhajipur garbage dump into a park. When someone questioned what would happen to the garbage, it was decided to let it remain where it was—on roads, in overflowing dustbins, in sewers and just about everywhere.

Then came the second problem. Unknown to the housing department, people had built illegal houses on that dump. Removing them was a challenge. Getting an eviction notice from the court at short notice was impossible. It took years—the right to shelter, etc. to evict someone.

It required a different approach, and so another wily official, who was due for promotion, struck a deal with the gang-leader of the unofficial Bhajipur garbage dump housing society that an alternate location would be provided to them if they agreed to move their butts. It was a lie, but the leader signed when his palms were greased. Before the ink had dried on the agreement, the bulldozers razed the shanties.

Finally, the work began. Again, a foreign contractor was chosen, as none of the local contractors had the wherewithal or track record of completing projects on time. The park had to come up in four months so that it could be inaugurated two weeks before the elections. No expense was spared.

Machines were imported, and so were flora and fauna. The park was planned to have four entry gates—black gates with a golden border akin to Victoria Park. An open gym was created, as well as an artificial water body. A flagstaff was erected at the centre of the park, and during the inauguration, the then-CM unfurled the national flag. The project was a hit, and the Victoria Party won the elections.

That was ten years ago.

In the succeeding ten years, the Azaad Maidan had transformed back to where it originated from—a garbage dump. The squatters who were betrayed by their leader were back, and their leader's badly mutilated body was found a few days later. The wild vegetation had taken over the manicured lawns and flower beds.

The rough grass was knee high, and its razor-sharp edges could cut a person into pieces. The Gulmohar trees had become ancient; their eerie roots were now protruding from the soil. As such, the gym equipment and flagstaff were stolen a week after the inauguration. Now, the park was the favourite of junkies and squatters as the wild shrubs provided them with privacy.

The frame of concrete benches was eaten away by corrosion to the extent that these could not even take the weight of an infant. The park was littered with millions of empty cans, used condoms, and discharged batteries. The water body had been dried long back by people who washed clothes there, and now, there was just a layer of thick algae. Still, young urchins in dirty shorts occasionally braved to enter the park to play cricket, for lack of a better alternative.

Jagmohan was the magician of Azaad Nagar. His tent company—the Taj Mahal Tent House, was known to transform the filthiest of places into tolerable venues for marriages, naming ceremonies, *kirtans* and *chauthas*. As the entire AN was a dump yard, Jagmohan was much in demand, and his business had flourished over the years.

Early that morning, he was ecstatic when he got a call that his tent company had been selected to make arrangements for Guruji's rally at Azaad Maidan. No money was discussed because he deciphered from the caller's tone that none would be offered. But then the caller did say that if done well, opportunities would open up in Victoria.

To work in Victoria was Jagmohan's dream, so he got on his scooter and reached Azaad Maidan nice and early. He was told that time was of the essence and everything was to be completed by noon before Guruji's arrival. Initially, his excitement knew no bounds, but he was unsure an hour later. The park was so ramshackle that he had never seen any place as filthy before. That was an assessment from someone who specialised in building Taj Mahals over sewers.

His team had arrived in a tempo and were now huddled together, smoking bidis.

"*Behenchods*, get on with the work," he shouted with ferocity.

He had only four hours before Guruji's arrival. He took a broom in his hand and started right away.

Approval

Commissioner Nand Kishore kept staring at the file. He had a clear-cut directive from the CM that the request to conduct Guruji's rally at Azaad Maidan must be denied at any cost. Also, the roadshow was not to be allowed. "Cite the prevailing security conditions in the city, especially the burning down of the GCI factory."

In normal circumstances, there was not much to consider after the political master had given an order. But these were not normal times. The citizens were sharply divided over FLS, and there was an even chance that Siddheshwar Gupta could lose. On the other hand, Nand Kishore had two more years to go. If Gupta eventually lost, the next government may transfer him to an inconsequential position for this act. He had worked hard, licked many asses to become commissioner, and was not ready to risk anything.

As always, he needed advice. But what he actually needed was a shoulder to fire from—a scapegoat. He called Inspector Ganpule.

"Why has this application come to me?" He asked, looking at the file.

"Sir, because it's an important issue, only you can decide," Ganpule replied curtly.

"You know that is the problem with this department. No one wants to stick their neck out. Everyone keeps sending this up the chain."

Ganpule quickly understood his boss' game plan. He wanted him to come to his rescue, but he would not. He had finished a bottle in the night and was hungover, and desperately wanted to hit the bed. Nand Kishore poked his ear with the tip of the pen. The filthy habit apparently stimulated his thinking.

"Who is in charge of the Azaad Maidan area?"

"Pandey."

"Call him up and ask him if permission can be given."

Ganpule called Pandey and put the call on speaker.

Kya re? Pandey answered after three rings.

"Commissioner Sir wants to know if permission can be given for Guruji's rally at Azaad Maidan."

"*Behenchod*, tell that *chutiya*, I am investigating five murders and three rape cases, and I have not slept for days. I don't give a fuck about the rally," Pandey ranted and disconnected.

Nand Kishore turned red, but only for a few seconds. His thick skin was the catalyst for his career.

"So that means that permission can be given?"

"If you say so." Ganpule was enjoying this.

"What about the roadshow permission?"

"Let me get DCP Traffic."

"Ok, go outside and talk; no need to talk here, and never ever put the call on speaker in front of me."

Ganpule walked out of the commissioner's room, trying hard to control his laughter.

He returned after a minute. "Sir, he is saying that permission is to be granted or denied by you."

"Where is the deputy commissioner?"

"He is in his room."

Suddenly, Nand Kishore turned pale and started shivering. "Tell him I am not well and am going to the hospital. He will be officiating in the interim. Get the orders out."

Ganpule was expecting this. This was his boss' old trick. He also knew that the deputy commissioner would do the same thing. He looked at the file for some time. Someone had to write 'Approve' and sign.

Why couldn't he be that person?

He wrote, approved and signed with a flourish.

Roadshow

The atmosphere around Victoria Park was electric. The centre of attraction was the *rath* built on the Isuzu chassis, on which Guruji would cover the distance of fifteen km between Victoria Park and Azaad Maidan. One of the spins by the organisers was that the rich had repudiated Guruji while the poor had embraced him. It had nothing to do with FLS; instead, it was a class war that had been going on for centuries.

Tanvi and the other organising committee members had hurriedly prepared the plan for the roadshow. Leading the entourage as a vanguard was Tanvi Mehra in an open jeep. She was in a white salwar kameez, a red dupatta covered her head, and a large *chandan* tilak adorned her forehead.

The jeep belonged to Toni, who was in the driver's seat. He had come straight from Royal Salute, and his breath analysis would give his perception of power and capabilities equivalent to someone unconscious or in a coma. Tanvi didn't want him in the driver's seat, but he was insistent.

Her jeep was followed by five more jeeps, mostly with opposition leaders holding placards. The last one had Banke. He had wanted to sit with Guruji and had thrown a fit. "Just a few days back, I was Deputy CM. You can't treat me like this." But he was given an ultimatum that either it was that jeep or nothing. He sulked, but eventually complied.

Then, there were people from Gabru's village. They came in tractors. They blamed CM Siddheshwar Gupta for Gabru's death, and they wanted to seek revenge. Each tractor had a stock of around ten litres of liquor. Behind them were foot soldiers, thousands of them, in white Gandhi topi like Guruji's. There were also *dhol walas, bhajan tollis* and dance troupes. The loudspeakers tied to the frame of the jeeps belted out one patriotic song after another.

A large police force was present, but their hands were tied because the roadshow had the necessary permission. When the DCP on duty saw that approval was signed by an inspector, he tried to reach the commissioner.

"Everyone has diarrhoea," he was told by the operator. "Commissioner, deputy commissioner, and just about everyone in HQ."

There were two pilot bikes in front of Tanvi's jeep. Fattu was on one, and Lovely on the other. Despite Tanvi's request, Lovely had not relented. "If something happened to you, I would never be able to forgive myself," the Godfather had reasoned.

There were a few strategic halts planned for the roadshow. The first one was in front of the Kapoor villa. Since GCI was the direct beneficiary of FLS, it was logical to protest in front of its promoter's house. Tanvi raised her right hand when her jeep was abreast of Kapoor villa, and the procession stopped. On cue, the paid protestors started shouting, "GCI *haye haye.* GCI *haye haye."*

Then, as was directed, a few pelted stones, which they were carrying in plastic bags. One broke Soundarya's bedroom window pane. Fattu got so excited and agitated that he left his bike, ran towards Kapoor villa, and started climbing the boundary wall. He wailed when the shards of glass on top of the wall cut his hand.

Chutiya-Lovely laughed at him when he returned to his bike. Tanvi was silently watching the *tamasha*. She knew that Soundarya was living in Diplomat, but then she noticed Rameshwaram leaning on the terrace and recording. She looked at him and showed him the finger, sure that it would be transmitted to Soundarya seconds later.

The next stop was the CM office. Here the slogans changed to, "GKP *haye haye.* GKP *haye haye.*"

However, there were strict security arrangements, and police did a *lathi charge* on protestors who tried to come close to the CM's building. Tanvi wanted to move fast from there lest the situation escalate, but then she saw something which made her both scared and excited.

The protestors from Gabru's village, who till now were driving their tractors in a disciplined straight line, suddenly went berserk. They were here to protest against the CM, if possible, to kill him and gave two hoots about FLS. One of them took his tractor at full speed and rammed it into the main gate of the CM secretariat.

Another drove to the footpath and destroyed the tea stall where *babus*, working in the CM secretariat, drank tea. Then there was one who was piss drunk. He lost control, and his tractor started going in circles. He would have killed a few had his tractor not overturned.

The CM was watching everything from his third-floor office window and cursing the moment he had agreed to Meenakshi Tandon and introduced FLS. Finally, Guruji had to use a loudspeaker and ask the protestors to move on.

The third protest site was the *Dhobhi* Colony toll—the gateway to Azaad Nagar. Here, the stone pelting did take place, but the target was the procession. A stone even hit Guruji's rath. Guruji was taken inside the cockpit, where he continued sitting for the rest of the journey.

From then on, it was like that. Flowers were showered on the procession at a few places and stones at some. All in all, the situation was clearly described by a political pundit in his tweet.

FLS: The poor begged, the middle class was clueless, and the rich didn't give a damn #mindthegap

By the time the procession reached Azaad Maidan, it was noon. Jagmohan and his team were bruised and sweating through all pores. They were hurriedly placing durries. Whatever was filthy was hidden by bunting cloth. The pond was covered by a tarpaulin. A shamiana was erected at the centre, and four rows of gaudy chairs were arranged. Considering everything, Jagmohan had done a great job, though he couldn't do anything about the smell of faeces.

The government people who came to put cameras were driven away, and liquor was given as an award to their attackers. The *bhajans* started at 1 pm.

Ananya Dutt tweeted at 4 pm, "Tanvi Mehra has shown that she has nerves of steel. The way she has played the game and made everything boomerang on Siddheshwar Gupta is incredible. The show continues at Azaad Maidan."

At 5 pm, Tanvi Mehra was arrested.

Interrogation

"How dare you give the permission?" Nand Kishore hollered. He was back in his chair and had sent a message to the CM that he was not involved in the decision-making for the rally and that there was some confusion. "I have formed a fact-finding committee, and an exemplary punishment will be given to whosoever was behind it."

"Sir, you can suspend me," Ganpule challenged.

"*Arre nahi yaar*. We are a team. We are family," Nand Kishore said and showed his yellow teeth. He was glad that Ganpule had done the dirty work for him. Denying permission would have been suicidal. "What about Tanvi Mehra? Have you filed the charge sheet?" Nand Kishore was suddenly all business.

"What are the charges?"

"Section 153, arson; she was behind the fire in GCI factory."

"I don't have any evidence of that, do you?"

Nand Kishore gritted his teeth, but restrained his voice. "Find out, Ganpule. Please interrogate her and find the evidence."

Ganpule had seen Tanvi Mehra on TV and had developed an instant dislike. She came across as insincere and someone exploiting Guruji for selfish reasons, just like Siddheshwar Gupta had done five years back. But then he had to do as told, so he called the jail superintendent and asked him to get Tanvi Mehra to the interrogation cell.

Half an hour later, she was sitting across from him, wearing the same white salwar kameez she had worn when she was arrested from

Azaad Maidan. Barring a few strands of hair that had gone astray, she looked calm and composed, as if sitting in a conference room for a business meeting. This irritated Ganpule, and he decided to pin her down quickly.

"So, you are the one who burnt the factory?" He asked abruptly.

"What are you talking about? I was in the hospital. I am sure you would have done some homework before coming here," Tanvi fired back.

"That is a frivolous alibi. You didn't do it yourself. You got it done, just like how you ignited the fire that killed Gabru."

"Your false allegations will not dampen my resolve. Hang me if you want, but I will continue agitation against FLS till my last breath," Tanvi replied calmly.

Though she said it sincerely, there was something acidic in how she replied, and Ganpule gathered that he was dealing with a shrewd woman who would not yield easily. It would require a lot of tact.

"How are you connected to Soundarya Kapoor?"

"She is a friend, or rather, she was."

"What happened? Didn't you both run that M&S *chutiyapa*?"

Tanvi laughed. "Don't call it that. It is the most sought-after group in the city. Even your commissioner wants to be a member. You can also join. Just have to ask me."

Tanvi's eyes were penetrating Ganpule's as if she, not him, was the interrogator. She found him attractive. Under his simple facade, she could sense raw masculinity, like those who were unaware of their own power or deliberately tried to hide it from the world.

Good god, what was she thinking? She was in jail.

"I understand you had a fallout with her. What the fuck happened?" Ganpule said more firmly than he had intended. He wanted to wipe that smug smile off her face.

"I became a victim of her insecurities," she said, maintaining her countenance.

"What insecurity?"

Despite her calm demeanour, Tanvi's mind was racing. She sensed that she would have to open up to explain her motives. She also suspected that Ganpule was the kind of man who would appreciate honesty.

"We were childhood friends. Both of us lived in Azaad Nagar. I was from a middle-class family, and well, she was poor. Somehow, we found each other in school and developed a friendship. Over the years, our friendship grew, and we became best friends. Do you know what happens when someone becomes your best friend?"

"What?"

"Jealousy strikes. I was far more popular than her and got better grades. I was an extrovert, whereas she just couldn't open her mouth for anything. In reality, she was my friend because I could show off in front of her. She always cheered my exploits and achievements, and at some point, I developed a superiority complex.

"I started seeing my successes as her defeats until suddenly, she knocked me down one day by marrying Kiku Kapoor. She became rich and powerful overnight. We lost touch for many years, and then, one day, we met, and our friendship rekindled. However, now the situation had reversed. I was still in Azaad Nagar, and she had become a Victorian. She had won, and I had lost. Do you know what happens then?"

Ganpule shrugged his shoulders.

"You start hating your friend."

"But then you were together."

"I was because it gave me a second chance to win the race, and she was because she wanted to constantly rub it in that she had won.

Now, I had become her cheerleader. But still, she was good to me in public, but hated me privately."

"So, it is all about your twisted sensibilities. You are willing to kill people just to get even. Do you know how sick you are? You need a psychiatrist."

"Not anywhere close to how much Soundarya is."

"This agitation is a result of your personal ambition. Am I right?"

"Yes, it is. I don't care a fuck about FLS. In fact, I love my drinks," Tanvi confessed.

"You haven't told me why you fought?"

"It happened two weeks back. It was my birthday, and I threw a lavish party. I borrowed a lot of money to organise it. I was the centre of attention, and everyone was loving it, except for one person. I could sense that she was looking at me with hate-filled eyes. Then, just before the cake-cutting, she walked out and forced the whole of M&S to leave with her.

"The next day, she removed me from the group. My own fuckin group, the one I had created. In hindsight, she was not only insecure about my rising popularity but also because of her financial problems, and I will make sure that her worst nightmares come true," Tanvi hissed.

"Are you serious? Are you really fighting for this shit?" A puzzled Ganpule asked.

"People are wired to envy and despise others. These things may seem superficial to an observer, but ask someone who has lost everything, even the desire to live, because of humiliation. I was on the verge of committing suicide. If FLS is the last hope for Soundarya to survive, I will ensure it never sees the light of day."

"But it's already a law."

"There are many a slip between the cup and the lip."

"Who is helping you?"

"I guess some divine force."

"But all this is attributable to you. You will be in jail forever and even hanged."

"Says who? If someone feels strongly about the cause and does something, how can it be attributed to me? By your logic, Guruji is also guilty. Anyway, you will soon meet my divine force."

"How?"

"Because they will come to get me out. *Mere Karan Arjun aayenge.*"

The Shot Is Ready

As the treadmill raced at the speed of twelve, she started taking stock of the situation. Tanvi's arrest was good news, though it had also made her nervous because Tanvi was more dangerous when pushed to the wall.

But that was not her only reason for worry; the other was the actions of Sumitra Kapoor, who was going berserk in sending messages to all and sundry that Soundarya had usurped the chairmanship of GCI by unfair means and also that there was something fishy in her son's death.

Both allegations were true, but then the truth could not be allowed to jeopardise plans, especially when victory was near. She had to be controlled, or else an investigation may start that could threaten the award of FLS tender to GCI. Soundarya also feared that the scope of the investigation may extend to the circumstances under which Kiku Kapoor died.

The Kapoor family had a history of arrhythmia, and that's why no one had raised an eyebrow when Kiku Kapoor died of heart failure. But someone who probed deeply would find out that days before his death, Kiku, instead of taking adrenaline-reducing beta blockers, was taking adrenaline-enhancing steroids.

The only way to damage control was if Sumitra Kapoor denied making those allegations. She finished her run, and after following her set weight training routine, she called Rameshwaram. An hour later, Soundarya arrived at Kapoor villa and proceeded to Sumitra's ground-floor bedroom, where she knocked on the door. A nurse answered, and Soundarya instructed her to leave.

Her mother-in-law was sleeping.

"*Maaji,*" Soundarya called out.

No response. She shook her leg. No response. She signalled to Rameshwaram, who poured water into his palm and sprinkled it on Sumitra's face. Sumitra's eyes opened, and she sprang up in panic. She looked at Soundarya as if she had seen a ghost.

"Namaste *Maaji.*"

Sumitra didn't reply.

"Why are you here?" She finally asked after gaining her bearings.

"*Maaji,* I have come to you with a request, and as always, it is not about me but our company. GCI is on the verge of getting the biggest order in its history, but your messages could spoil everything."

"They are all true, and soon, you will be behind bars," Sumitra whizzed.

"Nothing of the sort would happen, and you know that," Soundarya said and laughed.

"Why are you here?" Sumitra asked.

"I am here to do damage control so that this crisis can be avoided. All you have to do is make a statement that you never said those things and that you and I have the most cordial relationship. You have to say that Soundarya is like my daughter and best suited to run GCI. Then we will click some pictures together.

"I have an excellent journalist waiting outside who will soon come up with a nice cover story of how much we love each other and how Kiku's death has brought us closer. Of course, we must first clean up the living and dining areas. I have already asked the cook to make your favourite *gobi parathas,* which I will feed you with my hand."

Instead of replying, Sumitra closed her eyes. Once again, Rameshwaram sprinkled water, this time much more than last time. An enraged Sumitra sprang up from the bed and charged towards Rameshwaram.

Badtameez.

"Say sorry to *Maaji,* how dare you," Soundarya shouted simultaneously. Then, she addressed Sumitra, "*Maaji,* he is a crazy person. He listens to me, but then he won't if he sees that I am getting hurt. So, please do as I say," Soundarya said and folded her hands.

"Over my dead body," Sumitra hissed.

"*Maaji,* life is a gift, and you have many years left. I will make sure that you always have this house to live in. But more importantly, I know you would like to take revenge on me. Sooner or later, you will get your chance. So, why not wait to live another day. If you don't, you will be forever gone in the next minute."

Sumitra Kapoor just stood there, scared and shaken. She knew the threat was real.

Moments passed before she said, "Can I have privacy to change my clothes?"

"Oh, of course."

A few minutes later, Soundarya knocked at her door. "*Maaji,* the shot is ready."

Victoria Jail

Even though both were jails, the one in Victoria was far better than the one in Azaad Nagar. The Azaad Nagar prison was not only overcrowded but also had poor sanitation conditions, and inmates regularly endured physical and sexual abuse. Many died before their term ended. In contrast, the Victoria jail was more like a correctional facility reserved for politicians, celebrities and industrialists. It had recreation spaces, a decent library, and even a makeshift conference facility for the rich to conduct business.

But despite the luxury afforded to its prisoners, the Victoria jail was a high-security facility. An eight-foot perimeter wall protected the five-acre prison. Day and night cameras were located every fifty metres, and the video footage was fed to a central command centre manned twenty-four seven.

There was only one operational gate in the facility to facilitate the movement of men and materials. It was defended by boom barriers and armed guards. 'Trespassers would be shot' was prominently written on the board affixed to the gate. Therefore, under its laissez-faire guise, the Victoria jail was virtually impregnable.

His mind told him that there was no need to take a risk. Tanvi would be released sooner than later. But then his heart told him something else—*what was the point of being the top gangster if he couldn't rescue his girlfriend?*

But then, prison break became fait accompli when he received a phone call from her. She had spoken in a scared voice, "They may just keep me here for the rest of my life," and Lovely felt her pain and tears. After she disconnected, Lovely's blood boiled in rage, and he broke the windshield of a random car parked on the street.

After that, the Ghatak gang set into motion the most daring mission in its history. They spent hours brainstorming—could they enter the prison posing as delivery boys? It was way too risky. The latest sketches released by the police closely resembled them. The other option was to breach the perimeter, but they would have to somehow fool the cameras.

"Can we make a camera blind?" Fattu came up on his fourth drink.

"*Matlab?*" Lovely asked.

"Just like how we can make a person temporarily blind by pointing a torch at his eyes."

They googled and learnt about 'flash blindness', and after some more browsing, found that even cameras could be made blind. A heavy-duty laser torch could do that. They found a supplier on the web and sourced one. En route, they also gave measurements for the constable uniform and warned the tailor to make it ready in a couple of hours or be prepared to face the consequences.

Then, they encountered another problem while detailing the operation. One had to continuously point the laser at the moving camera lens, which was impossible if both had to climb a rope to get inside. The same thing had to be repeated during their escape. Lovely told Fattu that he alone would go inside while Fattu stayed outside with the torch.

Fattu took it as an insult and point blank refused, "Bhai, I will never let you do it alone." Lovely tried again, but Fattu was firm in his decision. "*Jai-Veeru* will do it together." After some to and fro, they decided that Ghatak needed to hire another member.

When they had started Ghatak, Lovely and Fattu were clear that it would only be two of them—*Teen tikada kaam bigada*. But now, they had to recruit one more, someone who could be trusted.

They screened many candidates, from pickpockets to murderers, but could not find anyone with the assurance of unconditional loyalty. Lovely had almost given up when his mind wandered to the day he had dropped out of school. It was then that he remembered Kaalia. In an instant, everything became clear to him. There would have been no Ghatak if Kaalia hadn't been caught cheating that day.

Kaalia was an innate member of Ghatak.

A few phone calls later, Fattu found out that Kaalia had also left schooling that day, but instead of trying something exciting, he had become a casual labourer and was working for daily wages under the guaranteed employment scheme of the government. When Fattu called him, he was digging a road in some part of the city. In the next half an hour, he resigned and was standing in front of them.

In school, everyone called Kaalia, Daku Mangal Singh, a popular dacoit in movies with a face that resembled a bulldog. Anyway, his family had named him Kaalia because of his skin colour. He was also short and stout.

After their team was completed, they went into detailed planning. They decided to breach that part of the perimeter abutting the crematorium. Kaalia would keep the car ready when they brought Tanvi out. They inspected the ropes and the hooks and did some dry runs on a public toilet wall. As he was a little slow, Kaalia was made to operate the torch a hundred times.

They made their move at midnight. They walked the length of the *kabrastan* and took a position near the prison wall. Kaalia pointed the laser at the camera while Lovely and Fattu threw the hooks on the top of the wall. After a few attempts, the hook was firmly placed, and they both started climbing up and then quickly climbed down on the other side. They were relieved that the lights on internal peripheral roads were off.

They smoothened their constable uniforms and started walking confidently. If someone would have noticed them, the first impression would be that they were security sentries. After walking around a hundred yards, Lovely noticed the circular roof water tank which Tanvi had mentioned. She had said she was kept in that building, and her cell was second on the right side of the entrance.

Lovely could not contain his excitement. With a burst of energy, he sprinted the remaining stretch and approached the gate that marked the entrance to the second cell. Even if Tanvi had some doubts about their future, they would all get eliminated after he rescued her. He started humming a song about undying love.

He entered the building gate. He was unconscious a few seconds later.

The woman who had taught him the art of seduction had now taught him the art of betrayal.

Breaking News

27 December

The central government has severely reprimanded Siddheshwar Gupta for the law-and-order situation in the state. Our sources tell us that president's rule is being considered.

All liquor shops remained closed today to protest FLS. The shop owners fear that FLS would put them out of business.

As per the latest Mood of the Nation survey, V-AN Happiness Index is at an all-time low.

Introspection

V-AN was a characterless city. There was no glue, no common thread, which held people together. They spoke diverse languages, ate different food and looked different. Most were migrants, and even after staying in the city for decades, they had never made a connection. For them, V-AN was a prostitute to be fucked and not loved.

It was initially a union territory. Then, after years of struggle by politicians, it became a state. Those who wanted it to become a state had ulterior motives. A state is a better fuck. The ordinary people didn't give a fuck one way or the other.

But even after obtaining statehood, the central government's appointed governor had a lot of say in the affairs. His seal of approval was required for any decision taken by the state government. Siddheshwar and the governor never got along, and not without a reason.

Every single decision Siddheshwar took was challenged by the governor, and only after a prolonged tussle in the media and courts did anything get implemented. Lack of trust was an understatement; they hated each other so much that they had not met for over a year despite the provision of a weekly meeting between them.

Siddheshwar had often spoken against the governor in public. "Governor is not my headmaster. People have elected me as chief minister." The GKP party workers had burnt the governor's effigy many times, and protests in front of LG's house was a daily occurrence. Similarly, the governor also made scathing remarks against the GKP government at every opportunity.

There was already a buzz in political and media circles about what the governor's take on FLS would be, though there was precedence on the governor's role in decision-making on welfare schemes. When the government had brought in FEWS, the governor had shot down the scheme until the court had reprimanded him, "Governor can only take action on land and public order issues."

The decision on FLS was an easy one for the governor. It was an issue of public order. The state's peace, calm and security were under threat. He smiled while making a written reply to Siddheshwar's 'Request for Approval' on file:

Your proposal to implement FLS has brought the city to its knees. Wherever I see, a fire is burning, and people are dying. Guruji, an old god-like man, is fasting in protest. I am extremely pained that even after all this, your government is hell-bent on implementing this flawed scheme, which has divided society like never before. Under the powers vested in me under Section 166 of the constitution, I hereby disapprove the FLS.

Further, I also urge you to reflect on your conscience. You came into public life as a crusader against corruption. See what you have become!

He returned the file to the CM secretariat, but not before leaking his note to the press.

***

Although it was not unexpected, the governor's note stung Siddheshwar rather severely. He removed the note from the file, tore it into bits, and threw it across the table on the face of the messenger. What hurt him the most were the last two sentences. There was no requirement to write that.

The governor was no saint. He had a chequered past and was involved in multiple corruption cases. For him to give a moral lecture was a height of hypocrisy. He feared that he would have leaked his reply to the media, and soon it would be a 'Breaking News'. His premonition came true immediately as dramatic music on the TV brought a flurry of breaking news.

FLS Rejected by the Governor

Governor asks Siddheshwar Gupta to introspect.

"In a big blow to GKP, the governor has outrightly rejected the FLS. We are getting the first reactions from former minister Bhure Prasad, 'This is the beginning of the end'."

"We have approached the court," said the law minister.

"We are reporting live from Azaad Maidan, where the protestors are singing and dancing joyfully."

"Today, Gabru's soul has rested in peace."

"Highways are blocked, and stone pelting incidents have been reported from various parts of Azaad Nagar."

"A youth leader of GKP will self-immolate in protest against the governor's decision."

"Only sellers in GCI stock."

CM knew there was only one way out of this mess, and he knew who could deliver it. He called him up.

Narcissist

The look of betrayal on his face haunted her. His screams and the way he had furiously resisted when he was hit by the guards had made her tremble. All that had happened in front of her. Only after Inspector Ganpule had pounded his temple with the butt of his revolver did he faint, and finally, the screams stopped.

She had no guilt or emotions towards a criminal who had fallen for her. But she was scared as hell. She was sure Lovely would kill her in a heartbeat if he ever got free from jail. Betrayal is often the prime motive for revenge, especially if you believe your lover betrayed you. It is then the animal instincts take over.

She had struck a deal with Ganpule. She would sacrifice her *Karan* and *Arjun* in exchange for her release. The only gamble she took was that Lovely may spill her name as a mastermind when interrogated. But then she had immense confidence that a fan of the Italian mafia would never snitch his lover.

Will he be in jail forever? She hoped so for her own sake.

She finished her breakfast, which was surprisingly good. Twenty-four hours in jail was not all that bad. She had made acquaintance with fellow prisoners, one of whom was serving a term for corporate fraud. The other was accused of running an extortion racket. Both were refined and well-spoken. They had even played poker together.

Lost in thoughts, she lit a cigarette when a guard came and informed her that she had a visitor. She stubbed the cigarette and followed him. When she reached the visitor room, she saw Bhoomi Pracharak hunched on the chair, biting his nails.

She had learnt that Siddheshwar Gupta had ordered raids on AAM channel offices last evening. The narcissists wilt down quickly because, under all the false bravado, they are hollow. Just a few hours after raids, its owner and editor-in-chief was a sorry shadow of his previous self. His suit was full of creases, and his shoes were unpolished. Right then, it was difficult to imagine that he was the man who character assassinated and damaged reputations at the drop of a hat. He was a tiger under political patronage, and the moment that vanished, he had turned into a cow.

"You don't look too well," Tanvi enquired, feigning concern.

"Slight fever," he lied.

"Is this fever because of the raids?" Tanvi gave a knowing smile.

Just like a child cries when his mother touches a raw nerve, Bhoomi started howling at the mention of raids. "I did so much for Siddheshwar Gupta. Even when he was unknown and just an ordinary member of an anti-corruption gang, I was the one who brought him under the limelight and made him a political hero. See now what he has done to me. My office has been sealed, and it's a matter of time before AAM is taken off the air. The channel which I built with my blood and sweat is dying."

"But why are you so scared of raids? Do you have skeletons in your cupboard?" Tanvi feigned concern, though she was enjoying it.

"Who doesn't? Everyone in this city has. I have also done a few things in business, but that is not what I am scared about."

"Then what is it?"

"There's a tape of mine."

"Doing what?"

"An editor's life is stressful, especially in this era of Breaking News. I needed an outlet, and that outlet was Panache. It was always normal massages, but the day before, she offered more, and

I couldn't say no. I was foolish to fall into a trap. If this video comes out, I am finished, both personally and professionally."

Tanvi was thinking. She had to give the credit where it was due. Soundarya Kapoor was brilliant. She was sure Ruchi Sharma would use those pictures of her at the right time. But then Soundarya would know that they were useless. Tanvi Mehra could not be blackmailed with frivolous stuff, but this joker could.

"What can I do about it?"

"There are your pictures as well."

"It doesn't matter to me. There are thousands of pictures like this on the internet. I will just call it fake."

"But they have a way to prove that these are not." He was bewildered by Tanvi's casual response.

"It still doesn't make a difference to me."

"There is an offer for you directly from the CM."

"Is he in a position to give me an offer? FLS is dead. I have won," Tanvi dismissed him.

"Anyway, at least hear the offer," he pleaded.

"What is it?"

"You will be Deputy CM in his next cabinet."

"He still thinks he can win. I am surprised." Tanvi laughed.

"There's one way all can win."

"And what is that?"

"Convince Guruji to cease his fast."

A shiver of excitement ran through her body. This was the moment she had been waiting for. This was the time when *Khalnayak* broke the back of *Nayak*. Suddenly, the events of the fortnight unfolded in her mind. She remembered that fateful night two weeks back when she had lost everything. In just two weeks, she had reversed everything. She had a sudden urge to call Ashok and tell him that the hawk had got its prey.

Even though she was joyful, she didn't show it. This was the most exciting part and had to be savoured.

"I am fully invested in the cause. I respect Guruji too much to make him withdraw. Regarding Deputy CM, the Victoria Party has already offered me the CM's chair."

"If FLS goes through, Siddheshwar Gupta will win."

"Maybe, but if it goes through and you know, the governor has killed it."

Bhoomi was so taken aback with her casual replies that he decided that this was the time to show his manhood. He gripped Tanvi's left hand on the table and threatened in a voice laced with anger.

"Stupid bitch, stop playing these games! I will ensure you remain in jail for the rest of your life."

Tanvi swiftly brought the cigarette in her right hand and pressed it into Bhoomi's. His scream was heard throughout the building.

"I beg of you," he said, with tears rolling down his cheeks as he licked the burn with his tongue.

"Get out."

"Please."

"I said, get out."

As he slowly got up from the chair, she said in a low voice, "I need money, Hundred crores."

He quickly sat back. "It will be done. Do we have a deal?"

"Money is one part. I want something else as well."

"What is it?" Bhoomi was excited, like a bitch in heat.

After telling him what she wanted, Tanvi thought, *men are so easy to fuck.*

Motherland

Finally, a moment comes that one fears the most. Until then, one clutches at straws and clings to hope. Although she always knew what Tanvi ultimately wanted, the call from Siddheshwar Gupta still came as a surprise. Everything had changed in a fortnight.

The question was if she should fight on or give up.

She was unsure, but then there were some practicalities to be considered. She had built up a huge inventory of Gulaabo for FLS, backed by debt. FLS was her trump card, her ticket to survival, and without it, GCI and Soundarya Kapoor would cease to exist.

She was experiencing overwhelming hurt and anguish. She felt that, at that point, the entire world was mocking her.

She was weighing her options when her secretary called to inform her that Robert Brown was waiting for her at Royal Salute. He had called her several times and was desperate to meet her. She had no intention of seeing him, but he texted that he was coming down to Diplomat, and she reluctantly agreed.

It was turning out to be a horrible day. She had missed going to the gym and had a nagging headache. She hurriedly changed into jeans and a white top and went downstairs to the bar. She could spot Robert Brown from afar. He wore a finely tailored black suit and was on his favourite gin-tonic.

Soundarya made way to his table and sat opposite him. No pleasantries were exchanged; in fact, nothing was said as they both gauged each other. A server came with the wine list, but Soundarya sent him away.

"Why are you not replying to my calls?"

"What is that you want to talk about?"

"What the fuck is wrong with your country? How the fuck can this governor overrule everything?" Brown shouted so loudly that several heads turned towards their table.

"This is how things are done here. We have the rule of law. What about your country?" Soundarya said in an even voice.

"The rule of law. Bullshit, you should have remained our colony forever."

"Let's not get into all this. What do you want from me?"

"Set things right immediately. We have an agreement. I also paid money to Meenakshi Tandon."

"Why don't you speak to her?"

"No one knows where that bitch is," Brown spat.

"I am finally asking. How can I help?"

Brown looked at her with menace. He took a large gulp of gin-tonic and brought his face close to hers. "You are as much a bitch as Meenakshi. I let her fuck with me, but I won't let you. If you can't pull this off, forget GCI, I will make you a waitress in a seedy bar where you will give blowjobs for tips."

Suddenly, Soundarya was fraught with a range of emotions. How easy it was for men to make a woman a prostitute. She had seen glimpses of Brown's personal life in his Instagram posts where he had projected himself as a loving husband and father to her two daughters, teaching them how to cycle and swim.

Many monsters lived behind the smokescreen of social media. He was the man who had humiliated her Kiku, a man who was a million times classier than him and who respected women. It was he who had killed her Kiku. She had a powerful urge to slap him on his face, but she had a better idea.

She picked up his gin-tonic from the table and threw it on his face. "You son of a bitch, the deal is off, never call me again, you asshole."

As soon as the words were said, he pounced at her, and she fell backwards and shouted. The staff at the Royal Salute rushed towards their table. Two bouncers held the back of Brown's collar and dragged him a few feet away. Soundarya asked the front office manager to call the police.

Half an hour later, Brown was taken to Azaad Nagar prison on charges of attempted rape.

An hour later, Soundarya finished fifty laps of the pool. She was feeling light and easy, and she had made her decision. It was essential to be alive to fight the battle some other day. She came back to her room and masturbated herself to sleep.

After waking up, she called Siddheshwar, "I will do as she wants, but you would have to do a thing for me."

"What is it!"

"Robert Brown has been arrested. He not only tried to molest me but also insulted our motherland. Make sure that he never sees the sun again."

An hour later, Soundarya added Tanvi to M&S. Then she drafted the message as instructed:

My dear Tanvi, you are an integral part of this group and the one who germinated the seed of M&S. There may have been an impression amongst people that I was the one running the show, but it was you all the way. We both have the same roots, and I must confess that you are far better than me in just about everything. I am thankful to God that our slight misunderstanding is now resolved.

I apologise to you, Tanvi.

Welcome back!

Tonight, the M&S year-end party will be the celebration of your homecoming.

Soundarya reread the message several times. She wanted to add something sarcastic, something acidic so that people could read between the lines that she was not surrendering, but she just couldn't come up with anything. Tired, she pressed the Send button.

Then, she cried like she had never cried before.

M&S Year-End Party

Tanvi got to know that she was back in M&S from the constant ringing of her phone.

After she was released by the police, she went straight to Guruji and touched his feet. The people erupted in applause when she appeared on the stage. "Tanvi *devi ki jai,* Tanvi *devi ki jai.*" She was amused by how suddenly 'devi' was suffixed to her name but nonetheless enjoyed the adulation.

After spending some time with her well-wishers and supporters, she finally opened the M&S group and read the message from her. Then she closed her eyes and savoured her victory.

***

Everyone clapped when Tanvi entered the party. Soundarya walked up to her and hugged her tightly. That was the Kodak movement, and suddenly, the band hit the high notes, the camera flashlights blinded everyone, and there was thunderous applause. Booze and narcotics flowed, and soon the M&S was rocking.

Toni came running to her and said in her ears, "I am leaving Moni for you."

Another son of a bitch, Tanvi thought before nodding her head. Tanvi again asked for tea, but stealthily added a double shot of vodka from the flask in her purse.

At midnight, Tanvi cut a cake and fed the first bite into Soundarya's mouth. Soundarya reciprocated and then said in her ears, "Bitch, you got what you wanted. Now, it's your turn to deliver."

Half-Mast

As she drove towards Azaad Maidan, she encountered conflicting emotions. The euphoria of exacting revenge and getting back M&S was fading by the minute, and trepidation of what lay ahead made her heart pound and hands shiver. Most of all, Soundarya's words were torturing her; how easily she had called her a bitch on her face, basically telling her that even after everything, she was a nobody. As always, she would give it back, but then, how long would this cycle of revenge continue?

She suddenly felt listless and fatigued. She could see people sleeping on footpaths, and for some strange reason, it invoked jealousy in her. She deliberately braked the car at a crossing to watch a mother and her three children sleeping under the streetlight. There was something divine about how the children clung to their mother, who held them together, giving them warmth and comfort.

They may not have money, but they slept peacefully under the open sky while she was on the verge of making a windfall and felt hopeless and depressed. Suddenly, she felt a deep sadness that she didn't have any. Maybe having children would have made her humane.

I wish to sleep like them.

Fires were lit at many places at Azaad Maidan, and the motley crowd present was sleeping under its warmth. She took the car to the back entrance, where she was waved in by the private security guards. The regular police were absent. Even the regular nurse was missing, and the door to Guruji's makeshift restroom was opened by a new face.

She tiptoed to his room and saw that even Guruji was sleeping peacefully, just like those on the footpath, and she was struck by an epiphany—only a clear conscience led to peace.

This was the time for her to walk away from everything. This was her chance for redemption. To get her peace and, as always, she let it pass and instead, shook his legs to wake him up.

His eyes opened, and he strained to look at her. He adjusted the pillow and wore his glasses before asking, "Tanvi *beta*, what are you doing here?"

"Guruji, I am scared. They have all come after me," Tanvi said in a quivering voice.

"Why, what happened? Don't be afraid. Sit down," he said calmly.

"They are going to kill me."

"Who are they?"

"The powers who want your fast to end, or else I will have to pay the price with my life," Tanvi said in a panic-stricken voice.

"Don't worry, nothing will happen to you; I have been getting these threats forever. In fact, call the press now, and we will tell them everything."

"You don't understand, Guruji. They are ruthless beyond yours and my imagination. For god's sake, break your fast and return to where you came from." Tanvi raised her voice in desperation and folded her hands.

Guruji looked at her for a few moments before reacting, "That I will not do. Five years back, I agreed to Siddheshwar and am repenting till now. I am not going to budge this time. Let them kill me."

"But what about me? Aren't you worried about me?" Tanvi replied angrily.

Guruji studied her face and said in a pained voice, "You can also die. I knew of your intentions the day you came to meet me. I agreed to come with you because I believe in the cause and also the power of goodness and its capacity to rub off on others. I was wrong. Your soul is impermeable."

"Guruji, please, I have a family."

"Your mask has slipped. You are drunk. I could tell the moment you entered this room. I don't want you to be a part of this movement. I don't want to ever see your face. You represent evil. You are a *Khalnayak*."

At that moment, everything became clear to her. The song that night was not a coincidence. She was indeed a *Khalnayak*. That was her identity, and however much she tried, she would never be able to let go of that identity, the basis of her existence.

There was a Plan B.

She acted swiftly and forced him down and thrust the pillow into his face. When she was sure that he was not breathing, she started counting. "1, 2, 3,"

She stopped at 60.

Breaking News

30 December

Guruji passes away in sleep. He was 86. He will be cremated at Victoria Crematory at 5 pm with full honours.

"I have lost my father," Siddheshwar Gupta has said.

"End of an era," said Bhure Prasad. The state flag will be flown at half-mast for twenty-four hours.

Tanvi Mehra withdraws Andolan. "Let the people's will prevail," she said. She has also joined the GKP. "Guruji, before leaving, directed me to strengthen Siddheshwar's hands."

FLS cleared. After taking suo moto cognizance of developments over the past twenty-four hours, the courts have directed the governor to approve FLS. The FLS will come into force from midnight of 31 December.

Gulaabo Night. A New Year Party—Gulaabo Night, will be organised by the government at Hotel Diplomat on 31 December. The party will be attended by people from all walks of life. The FLS will be officially rolled out by the Chief Minister at the dawn of the New Year.

GCI stock hits 52-week high.

Gulaabo Night

Even though the forceful phlegmy cough made him curse after every drag, Sanjeev Khanna could not stop smoking. He had quit the filthy habit a few years back, but today, the anxiety had triggered the relapse. That and the fatigue. He had laid awake the whole night despite the warmth of her naked body next to him.

Julia worked in the front office, and their affair had started the day he moved into the staff quarters after taking over as General Manager. She lived in the hostel for single women in the same complex, and the sparks flew during their dinner at the staff canteen, partly because he was a charming man and partly because he was her boss.

Now, as he watched his nubile girlfriend through his office window, coordinating the delivery of supplies in her maroon saree, which incidentally she had draped in front of him, there was only one worrying thought in his mind, "How will I endure this day?"

Handling events was no big deal for him. He had spent most of his life managing parties, marriages, business conferences, parties, kitties and such shenanigans and had the best resume for the job. He was, in fact, so devoted to his work that consequential neglect of his personal life had resulted in two divorces within a gap of two years.

He had no home to go to and no household responsibilities, so he immersed himself in hotel affairs. His work was his life, and he was committed to enhancing Diplomat's reputation and the major events could act like a catalyst. But not today's event.

'Gulaabo Night' was a disaster in waiting, and he had reasons to believe so.

He had become a hotelier because hotels, particularly the five and seven stars, catered to a certain class of people. The gentry who checked in or visited fine establishments like Diplomat were not overawed with luxuries and excesses. In fact, they consumed much less in opulent surroundings than they would typically do.

Let's say if it was a party of the top fifty Victorians, an experienced hotelier would usually cater for half the number and still be left with untouched food and wine. Over the years, he had observed that rich didn't like others to watch them eat, so it was just perfunctory food tasting, a nibble here, and a bite there.

They also left the parties early and took measured sips of wines and whiskies. He just wanted to serve such a class, people with blue blood in their veins. In fact, if he had his way, he would ban entry of *Azaad Nagarites* into Diplomat, including those who had somehow acquired wealth and were now living in Victoria. He secretly wished for a boundary wall between Victoria and Azaad Nagar, like the one between North and South Korea and the trespassers sent to the dungeons.

Therefore, 'Gulaabo Night' was not something he wanted to be a part of, leave alone organise. There were five thousand invitees, and the majority were from AN. The MLAs were given guests quota proportional to the population density of their constituency. As a result, the highest allocation went to MLAs of the most notorious slums, regarded as the most wretched in the world.

The No. 1 was Karamdooma, and the number 2 was Parbatgunj.

Imagine a crowd like that in Hotel Diplomat with lifelong pending hunger. To err on the safe side, Khanna had planned to cater for double the number of people, but he was still unsure.

He had also proposed two sets of menus—one for the VIPs and Victorians and the other for commoners. His proposal was shot down by his boss, who had directly got instructions from the CM's office. 'Politicians cannot be seen discriminating during the voting season'; his boss had cajoled him when he had asked for leave during protest. The only concession he got was that people from AN would be served Gulaabo rum in steel tumblers instead of Diplomat's regular crystal glasses.

"Yes, both can be thrown to hurt or kill, but the cut of the glass could be more lethal than the thud of steel," he had reasoned passionately with his boss, who in turn had given the same logic to the CM's PA Bhola Singh.

Another issue was the brand of liquor to be served. For commoners, it was Gulaabo, the brand they will start getting free from midnight. "But what about others, our regulars and VIPs? Will they ever come back if we serve them Gulaabo?" Khanna had challenged his boss. In the end, it was agreed that arrangements would be made in the Maharaja ballroom for VIPs and patrons, but this all would happen in a hush-hush manner.

Becoming GM of Diplomat was Sanjeev's mission in life. As a child, he had attended a marriage function in Diplomat and was star-struck. A course in hotel management followed by a twenty-year career in the industry, starting as a bellhop and rising to become GM of Diplomat, was a dream come true for him. In the last week, he had tried his best to not let the event take place in Diplomat because it could potentially destroy his career.

Besides taking up with the management, he had also instigated the influential regulars who visited the Royal Salute and Panache. "Diplomat is your private club, don't let its distinctive character be assassinated by those AN hooligans; they will deflower our beloved hotel," he had pleaded.

Nothing had helped, and the day of reckoning was here.

Partly agitated and partly tired, he stubbed the cigarette and was about to enter the bathroom to masturbate, his time-tested habit of relieving stress, when he heard the commotion at the service entrance. His assistant manager came running and informed him that people had stopped the truck carrying Gulaabo for the evening's function.

Later, he came to know that the looters were invitees to Gulaabo Night and had started assembling since 5 am at the hotel's gate. Since they were denied entry as the function was to begin twelve hours later at 6 pm, they had parked themselves on both sides of the road in front of Diplomat. They didn't want to wait that long and so, when they saw trucks carrying Gulaabo entering the hotel, they looted it to get their party going as soon as possible.

Sanjeev cursed loudly and then alerted the police control room through the walkie-talkie that the police had given to him so that he could send an alert for emergencies. Even then, by the time police arrived, the truck with around 5000 bottles was looted. By 10 in the morning, half the people who were supposed to attend the GKP night were piss drunk.

***

The thirteen-day religious mourning period was about to get over, but not for Sumitra Kapoor. Losing her only son, the one she loved the most in the world, was devastating, but what she rued the most was that she could not save him in the end. Her son was physically and mentally weak and needed her protection from the tyrants of the world, and all her life, she had played the role of a protector.

She had fought with the mothers of bullies who had teased her son in school, her husband who hated their only son, her daughters who were always mean to him, and countless others who took advantage of his genial behaviour. But in the end, she had failed. How much ever she tried, this sadness and guilt would not leave her until her last breath. She just knew it.

She wanted to approach the law but was afraid of Soundarya. Her daughter-in-law had emerged extremely powerful and had the government's backing, and now, with FLS in force, she was virtually invincible. The other day, she was on the verge of killing her before she agreed to her demands, including clicking smiling pictures with her, which were splashed in the media, giving the impression that all was well between them. Her daughter-in-law was ruthless.

Her surroundings had changed in the last thirteen days. The Kapoor villa was slowly decaying with each passing day. It looked decrepit and abandoned. She could see from the window that the lawn now had long uncut grass, and weeds were mushrooming unchecked. The hydrangeas had started withering, and the main gate was rusting and made a creaking sound. Her favourite gardener, Rohtas, had run away, possibly under threat from Rameshwaram, who had suddenly become everyone's boss.

The *gunga* had become the man of the house, deciding everything from what was to be cooked to what was to be cleaned. Only he had access to Soundarya's room on the first floor, and she had seen him carrying suitcases in and out of her room. Whenever their eyes met, he looked away with a smirk. Once, she had mustered the courage to confront him but got scared thinking about the fury he could unleash.

Soundarya left the Kapoor villa the same evening Kiku died, but not before ensuring that her mother-in-law was kept under house arrest. She was not even allowed to attend her son's *chautha,* which took place in a nearby Gurudwara, because the doctor didn't consider her mentally fit. She was virtually locked in her room. A nurse was always on duty and gave her antidepressants and checked her blood pressure every couple of hours.

Soundarya's taking over as the chairman of GCI was a well-planned coup. She was neither the majority shareholder nor had the consent. Sumitra had even secretly made calls to the company lawyers and secretaries, and even though they were sympathetic to her, they all sided with Soundarya out of fear. She even sent a message directly to Soundarya, asking her to at least return her 100 crores, but she did not care to reply.

Everything had backfired on her in a matter of two weeks. She had been planning to get Soundarya out of her son's life but ultimately, lost her son. She tried focusing on her next move to stop the tears from rolling out.

Last night, she had bribed the nurse with a gold necklace in exchange for the freedom to be alone in her room. She opened the almirah and took out the box Tanvi had sent for her. After noting the time on the invitation for Gulaabo Night, she took the cold 0.45 ACP in her hand and started practising.

She would not let her get away scot-free.

She would take revenge, and only then would she immerse her son's ashes into the Ganges.

***

Siddheshwar signed off the letter to the PMO asking for more funds, his seventh request in as many days. The first five requests were rejected with a one-liner fax—'You are advised to put austerity measures in place until your state's fiscal deficit is under control'. However, the sixth fax had an additional query—'Please provide details of the FLS'.

By a separate fax, he was informed that the CBI would investigate the circumstances leading up to Guruji's death. The autopsy report, which had concluded that the death was due to sudden heart failure, was also under scrutiny, and the forensic experts were interrogating the doctors involved.

The CM had consulted the constitutional experts. Most of them said that he had all the rights to implement FLS just like other states enforced 'Prohibition'. But they also informed him that such cases usually landed in courts and could linger on for months or years. In any case, he was not bothered. At least FLS had given him a fighting chance in elections, though the kind of support he had gathered a day after FLS was announced was now dwindling.

He was also surprised by the public's response to FLS. He had expected that some sections of the population, religious types and some NGOs may oppose it, but he had never imagined that even some industrialists and businessmen would as well. His childhood friend, now a leading shoemaker, told him that FLS would be disastrous for his business.

"My workers toil in inhuman conditions, so they can earn to buy booze in the evening. Remove that incentive, and there is nothing left." Another friend who ran a chain of vegetarian restaurants said that he feared his sales would suffer because people preferred meat after drinking. There was a representation by HNI's that they wanted champagne under FLS.

Then, there were other litigations. GCI was not the only liquor company, so the competitors had filed a case against the award of the contract to GCI without a tender. The news of the potential takeover of GCI by TWW had also leaked out. "He has sold the state to foreigners. They will make this city a city of drunkards," Bhure Prasad had said.

Meenakshi Tandon was still incommunicado, but he now and then imagined her sipping margaritas in the Bahamas, laughing at how she had made a fool of him.

He handed another letter to Bhola to fax and turned his attention to the TV debate, where the self-appointed experts were discussing the latest opinion polls. Bhoomi Pracharak had stopped appearing on the channel, and his place was taken over by someone who seemed to be shriller and shrewder.

"There are signs that FLS may not be as big a game changer as Siddheshwar Gupta had hoped. The tragic deaths of Guruji and Gabru have dented the scheme. Even though the police have classified the first death as natural and the second as tragic, suspicions remain, and now, the case has gone to the CBI."

"Son of a bitch," Siddheshwar mumbled and was about to switch off the TV when the latest numbers flashed on the screen.

Victoria Party – 40 per cent

GKP – 32 per cent

Others – 22 per cent

His phone rang.

"Hello."

"Sir, Commissioner Nand Kishore, this side."

"Bolo."

"Sir, a very large crowd has *gheraoed* Diplomat. We need the army."

Siddheshwar Gupta opened the last drawer of his table and took out a bottle of whisky. He poured himself a *patiala* and gulped it in one shot. He had been drinking heavily since Guruji's death, and that was the only way he was able to survive.

***

She had locked herself in the room for the last thirteen days. Today, for the first time since that fateful morning, she reluctantly stood on the weighing scale, something she used to do ten times a day in what seemed like her distant past life. To her horror, she had gained five, mostly on her face, and noticed a few strands of grey, but more than anything, she felt dirty inside and outside.

She was still in the same clothes in which she had killed him. Her co-tenant initially showed concern for a day or two, but she moved out when the stench became unbearable. The one-bedroom apartment had turned into a seedy bar. There were empty beer bottles, cockroach-infested pizza cartons, and cigarette butts scattered all over.

She was experiencing frequent nightmares in which he looked at her with tenderness and affection. But she could also see the pain in his eyes. He often said to her he still loved her despite everything. Many a time, she tried to make him angry at herself, a mean, cold-hearted bitch, a murderer, but he never changed his countenance.

She remembered that evening in Royal Salute when he had laid his heart bare before her. He had sobbed uncontrollably, speaking of his father's hatred, his wife's cold-heartedness and his children's indifference. He had also said that his end was near, probably not knowing that he was sharing his premonition with the agent of his death.

After the brawl with Robert Brown, his nose was bleeding, and he had deep cuts on his arms. But despite his condition, he was nice to her. He didn't ask for sex. Instead, he had held her hands, asking for love.

In return, she had killed him.

She didn't do it for money. Despite her ambition to have a fitness studio of her own, she was not the kind who would sell her soul for money. She did it because she was scared of Soundarya Kapoor. She was petrified when she threatened her with dire consequences if she refused. Her instructions were to make him exercise till he passed out.

There was no point feeling pitiful. She was done with mourning. Revenge was her only shot at redemption. She took out the packet of money given to her and burnt it. Then, she got rid of her clothes and stood under the shower for a long time.

***

The housing department moved very fast when it came to providing accommodation to the ministers. The minute they received the communication that Tanvi Mehra would be sworn in as the new Happiness Minister, the team of officials was at her home in *Dhobhi* Colony to help her shift to a government bungalow on Leafy Lane.

Tanvi took the news of the CBI enquiry with calm because she had a strong alibi. The official time of Guruji's death was 6 am, and at that time, she was live on TV on the popular 'Walk and Talk' show. Only a few knew her whereabouts between 3.30 and 4.30 am, and she was sure none of them were breathing at that moment.

She wore a red saree with a somewhat scandalous blouse for Gulaabo Night. God only knew when again she would wear a daring outfit in public. Bhoomi had truly brainwashed her into believing that women politicians must not reveal an inch of skin. She took out the Gucci necklace that Toni had sent for her. It was beautiful and expensive.

Since he had announced to her that he was leaving Moni, he had flooded her WhatsApp with love messages, including pictures of the Amalfi coast, where he was planning their honeymoon. Toni may have been a good catch in her previous life, but not any longer. In fact, association with him could damage her reputation.

Not Toni, definitely not Toni, but she was looking forward to meeting a young ambassador who wanted to discuss measures she would take as Happiness Minister and which he hoped to replicate in his own country. She checked his photo and blushed. Another thing that she wanted to do was to drink openly at the Royal Salute. She was fed up with steel tumblers and porcelain mugs.

Today, she had no worries about when to reach. Protocol-wise, she was much higher than Soundarya now, who would be there to welcome her with folded hands. Soundarya had saved GCI but ultimately lost her life's most important race.

She had also decided to leave M&S at midnight. It was now beneath her to be part of such a group. However, she would occasionally attend parties only if invited as the chief guest.

Should she call Ashok and give him the news? He probably already knew, just like everyone else, that Tanvi Mehra was going to be a minister. She pitied him, but then it was his destiny to remain a *dhobhi*, or else she would have ensured that every roof in the state had his company's solar panels. What a waste!

She had spoken to Inspector Ganpule several times since morning, requesting him to shift Lovely to the Azaad Nagar prison. "The Victoria jail is too easy for him to break. He has already done it once. He would kill me if he got out," she had pleaded.

Ganpule had said it was only possible after Gulaabo Night, as the entire police force was busy making security arrangements. She was also promised a Z+ security by Siddheshwar, but that would be possible only after her swearing-in. She thanked her stars that Fattu was also in jail, or else he would have tried to get his boss out.

Guruji came into her thoughts a lot. She had already planned to go to his village and inaugurate his statue. A similar one would be put on the lawns of the Happiness Ministry building. After all, he was an agent of happiness because FLS wouldn't have been implemented had he not died.

She had no remorse for killing Guruji.

She was an ensnarer.

She finished her makeup and took the stairs to get into the waiting car, which would take her to Diplomat. As soon as the car started moving, she saw Lovely's father standing at her window with folded hands. She didn't know why, but asked her driver to stop and rolled down the window.

Lovely's father looked drunk and had tears in his eyes. He came up to her and said, "Since you are a big person now, please help him. He may be a criminal, but he is good at heart. His mother has not stopped crying since his arrest, and she will die if he doesn't come home."

Before Tanvi could say anything, he handed her a cheque. "This is your security deposit." Then, he fell at her feet.

Tanvi didn't react, though she felt sad all the way up to the venue. When the car was about to reach Diplomat, she opened her purse to take out her vanity kit for a last-minute touch-up. It was then she saw it.

It was a cardboard box.

In it was a bloody finger.

And a note, "We are coming for you —G."

***

By noon, the number of people trying to get into Diplomat had increased to a lakh. The troops had arrived from the nearest cantonment to guard the hotel entrance, but even then, several hundred had managed to sneak inside.

Those who were unable to get inside started looting the nearby shops. The first target was obviously the liquor shops, but once those got emptied, the looters shifted their focus to food, electronics, clothes—whatever they could get their hands on.

Those who were drunk were the most lethal. They broke the storefronts, bus stands, dustbins, hoardings, etc. Whatever they couldn't break was burned. They clashed with police, and the wails of sirens could be heard frequently. In normal circumstances, such anarchy called for the imposition of curfew or at least Section 144, but doing that on the eve of FLS implementation would have been suicide. The political class just hoped that the situation would somehow come under control.

Sanjeev Khanna received the first panic call from Panache. Ruchi Sharma howled on the phone, "Drunks have entered Panache; they are forcing my masseuses for a massage. Do something before any untoward incident takes place."

The second one was from the swimming pool in-charge, who reported that drunk men had removed all their clothes and were bathing in the swimming pool. A call from the gym followed. Even the front lawns had passed out men napping.

The pop singer, Bika Singh, was to be the star performer of Gulaabo Night. He was of the same lineage as Gabru but was more practical and smarter and stayed away from drugs. Leading the dance troupe was Rakhi Balwant. Counting the musicians and the support staff, there were around a hundred of them.

They were given the entire third floor to rehearse. It was two in the afternoon, and they were all hungry. The lunch had yet to be laid. A hungry and angry Bika called Khanna and threw the choicest expletives at him. Sanjeev Khanna profusely apologised and then called the head chef.

"I am fuckin' leaving," Sam Miguel threatened even before Khanna could utter a word. The chef was the winner of the Oscars of the culinary world—'The Michelin star' and was the pride of the Diplomat.

"What happened?" Khanna asked.

"The buggers have stolen all the food from the pantry. Except for my dick, I can't cook anything else."

"Assholes," Khanna swore under his breath and then asked the supply chain manager to go to the market and procure stuff for the evening. "If we cannot feed them in the evening, they will chop off my balls. Take the army along with you and get whatever Sam wants for the evening. Also, arrange some *aloo parathas* for Bika and the party, or he will kill me."

The situation was now out of control.

Khanna called up Commissioner Nand Kishore, "Please send commandos."

Half an hour later, a helicopter was hovering over the Diplomat, and commandos were slithering down on the roof.

***

Malaika looked at herself in the mirror and was satisfied with the result. She had cut her hair blunt and coloured it with streaks of red and green. Her experiments with her makeup had worked, and now she was unrecognisable, at least at first glance.

Last evening, she had contacted Benny. He was the bartender at Royal Salute and had served them when she had gone there with Kiku. Benny recognised her immediately, and when she asked for a pass for Gulaabo Night, he came up with a better idea.

"Why don't you help me at the bar tomorrow? You will get the best view, and you can drink whatever you like on the sly. Later, we can even dine at Maharaja Banquet for the VIPs."

That was perfect. She somehow had a gut feeling that all the action would take place at the Royal Salute.

She had reached the hotel early in the morning before the crowds had started thronging Diplomat. Benny had given her instructions on making cocktails, which she had listened to intently like an obedient student.

"You have to be on your toes because, at Diplomat, we serve the *crème de le crème,*" he had said proudly.

At quarter past four, she was scrubbing the wine glasses and watching the havoc around her from behind the massive bar counter. She knew it was the beginning of the end.

Kiku's curse would finish them all.

***

Banke started despising Bhola from the day he first saw him. He was five years old when his mother ejected Bhola from her womb, and even after so many years, her painful screams that night often echoed in his mind. The next day, Banke tiptoed into her room and saw Bhola in the cradle.

His younger brother had a black spot between his eyebrows, as if he was wearing a *bindi,* and it was the *bindi* that caused hate at first sight. As Bhola grew, so did the bindi, and so did Banke's hatred.

There were other dissimilarities as well. Banke was strong and muscular, whereas Bhola was weak and frail. While Banke was popular, no one gave a second glance at Bhola. Banke would beat up Bhola for the slightest reason, and their parents would always side with their elder son, their pride, their Kohinoor.

It was just the second day of Bhola's marriage when Banke forced himself onto the new bride. He was so tyrannical and brash that he didn't even try to keep it a secret and maintained the illicit relationship till he started preferring men.

When Banke became an MLA and moved to Victoria, Bhola's wife pleaded with him to take them along, and they moved to the servant room in Banke's bungalow. This suited Banke, who used Bhola as a servant and his wife as an unpaid mistress. After the GKP tsunami, Banke became Deputy CM, and Bhola's wife once again pleaded with Banke to get her husband a proper job. Banke agreed and got Bhola appointed as PA to the CM.

Now, after so many years, he finally learnt that his brother made up in shrewdness what he lacked physically. His brother had silently endured years of humiliation and beating because he was waiting for his chance to take the ultimate revenge—a knockout punch.

The pictures clicked by Bhola had made Banke a political pariah. Guruji's movement was dead, and FLS was getting implemented. He was no longer a part of GKP, and the Victoria Party didn't want him. The bottom line was that he was a certified homosexual, and nobody wanted to touch him, even with a barge pole.

His phone beeped. It was a broadcast message from Bhola: *All MLAs are to reach Diplomat by 6.30, CM would arrive at 7, and latecomers would be viewed strictly.*

Madarchod, he blurted out.

Today, he would do what he should have done when he had first laid his eyes on the *bindi wala* rascal.

***

A sewerage system is a city's lifeline because everything would be floating in shit without it. Ironically, it does not get the attention it deserves. There are a few subject matter experts on sewerage because no one wants to be associated with shit, muck, grime and filth, except for the chosen ones whose duty is to clean gutters.

When Kaalia approached Fattu's father, he said no in no uncertain terms, "He is dead for us." Kaalia, with his limited IQ, tried to reason with him. When that didn't work, he tried his limited EQ, "He is your own blood."

When even that backfired, then Kaalia put his knife on his throat. "If he is dead for you, you are also dead for him."

Kaalia understood his responsibilities. He was the lone member of the Ghatak gang who was free. When the boss told him to keep a watch on Tanvi Mehra, he had entered her house disguised as a *kabaddi*. There were a lot of empty whisky bottles in all the nooks and corners of her home, and he had found an opportunity to slip the box into Tanvi's purse. This was his own initiative. His gang was facing a crisis because of her, and he wanted to forewarn her of what lay ahead.

The finger was his own.

This was his baptism into Ghatak.

The sewerage drawings were kept in an old decrepit building under notice for demolition. Fattu's father was among the few living beings who knew such a record existed. They navigated through old wooden almirahs covered with pigeon shit and reached the one with the required drawings.

Fattu's father carefully took the maps and spread them on the floor. He was careful because the paper was so brittle that it would have disintegrated into a million pieces if any undue force had been applied.

For the next half hour, Fattu's father studied the map with such concentration that Kaalia was impressed. Finally, Fattu's father said before walking off, "The gutter on Leafy Lane in front of the CM's house connects to the sewerage tunnel of the jail. But if you want to try this, you need to have tools to cut the gratings at every bend of the tunnel."

By 6 pm, Lovely and Fattu had managed to open the ventilation duct in their cell. They were lucky that a central air conditioning plant was recently installed in the Victoria jail after the persistent demands of politicians and businessmen who were regular visitors. The duct had screwed louvres, and they used spoons stolen from the kitchen to unscrew those.

A mile away, Kaalia entered the gutter in front of the CM's house, wearing a mask and welding goggles. He had a tool kit in his rucksack to break open any obstacle which would come his way. Any other person in the place of Kaalia would have died of the smell. Kaalia was only slightly uncomfortable for a few seconds, and after that, it was normal for him.

First, Fattu and then Lovely entered the ventilation duct, which was half a metre in diameter. They both were slim and faced no significant challenge. The vent led them to the air handling unit next to the administrative building. They broke the large fan at the end of the air trunking with bare hands and freed themselves.

It was already dark, but they had to be careful, especially since they were in prison clothes. Kaalia had told them there were four gutters in the jail, and they had to enter the one near the police quarters. That was a good 200-metre distance from where they were, so they both ran while intermittently crouching.

They were only fifty metres away when the cameras caught them, which triggered the floodlights and siren. The quick reaction team was alerted in seconds, and they could hear the fast-approaching footsteps and flashlights approaching them. It was going to be touch and go.

They reached the gutter, and when they pulled open the lid, the footsteps halted. The policemen could not take the repulsive stink. They covered their noses and took a few steps back.

They made their way into the tunnel, and after a couple of zig-zag turns of the filthy pipe, they saw Daku Mangal Singh standing there, holding a hammer and displaying his ultra-white teeth. Despite the unbearable stench and the muck on their bodies, they hugged each other.

Kaalia had already arranged a car for them near Leafy Lane. An hour later, they sat drinking in their hotel room. Gulaabo Night had already started, and the devastation around Diplomat was live cast on television. After taking a bath, they had changed into suits. Lovely and Fattu were impressed when they learnt what Kaalia had done to his finger. It was one more reason to kill her.

"But what purpose will it solve?" Lovely asked his comrades after he was half a bottle down. When they didn't reply, he continued,

"People like Tanvi Mehra, Soundarya Kapoor, Bhoomi Pracharak, and Siddheshwar Gupta are the symptoms of the rot in the society. Today, if we kill them, someone else will take their place, and this cycle will continue.

"They will rule, and people like us will remain their pawns. Rather, we should do something to shake the foundation of the establishment. Also, we must take revenge for the torture we endured in jail, the hell we saw in the sewer, and our Kaalia's finger. The time has come to change the rules of the game."

"What do you have in mind?" Fattu asked.

"Something like what Don Pablo Escobar did against police and political persecution."

***

"How can a wife leave her millionaire husband, especially the one who had always treated her with respect and dignity? I was or am a textbook husband," KD Dubey confided in the counsellor.

The couple's counselling session was fixed the day before Mrs Dubey had eloped with her lover. KD somehow had an inkling of the coming storm and had booked an appointment with a renowned marriage counsellor cum relationship coach cum spiritual healer credited for destroying many marriages. Since the money was already given, he had decided to attend the session alone.

Nobody knew if the counsellor was married, just like nobody knew if he had any qualification. He became well known because he claimed a fledging practice abroad before he came to spread his message in the motherland. He also wrote a weekly column in a lifestyle magazine, which many believed was ghostwritten, and many thousands followed his Instagram account in which he posted a reel every two hours about love, fear, faith and karma.

They were sitting across each other in his plush office with furniture made from expensive wood that emanated a soothing fragrance. The imposing floor-to-ceiling bookshelf had coffee table books on spirituality and the Kama Sutra. Two giant nude portraits hung under the spotlights, and Buddha chants—*Om Mani Padme Hum* played on Olufsen and Bang.

"This is a strange case. But isn't life full of mystery?" The guru said in a deep, throaty voice. When KD didn't reply, the guru asked in a conspiratorial tone, "How was your sex life?"

"As good as it can be after thirty years of marriage. There are not many surprises after that," Dubey replied hesitantly.

"Was she having an affair?"

"Suman is a level-headed woman. We never fought with each other. She stood by me even when I was charged with this country's biggest corruption case. We have all the money in the world. Why did she leave me?" Dubey said and fell on the healer's feet.

Soon, the tentative sobs gave way to crying.

"Anything happened recently?" The healer asked when Dubey had stopped crying after ten minutes.

Dubey narrated what had happened at the M&S party. How he had seen her dancing and how Toni had humiliated him by beating him in front of everyone.

"I think she felt shamed after seeing her husband beaten up, and this is her way of telling you to be a man."

"How?"

"She has only seen your good side. You are caring and respectful. But then, you will be surprised to know that a woman also desires to see a man's bad side. She wants to see the animal in him, and only then does she completely succumb to him."

***

Most of the members of M&S had checked into the Diplomat after the year-end party. They were all invited for Gulaabo Night by Soundarya Kapoor, who, as a primary sponsor, had a quota of a hundred guests. They had booked the entire eighth floor and were busy partying nonstop.

KD Dubey was among them. The counsellor had advised him to keep himself busy to forget the pain caused by his runaway wife. Against his better judgement, he had decided to bring in the New Year with the M&S gang. It was a bad call because Mrs Dubey had eloped with a member of M&S, and Toni, who had exposed his inadequacies to his wife, was there to put salt on his wounds.

During the afternoon party, he openly made fun of KD in front of everyone. "Dubey ji will play solo sports for the rest of his life." KD ignored the caustic remarks and continued drinking gin, much more than his usual quota.

Before the lunch party ended, it was decided that all the members of M&S would meet up at 6 pm and have a couple of drinks before attending Gulaabo Night.

After retiring to his room, KD set the alarm for five pm. Gin took over, and he quickly fell asleep, but woke up after a short while with a nightmare. In his vivid dream, he saw Suman and her new partner making passionate love. He was sweating despite the air conditioning and could feel heart pulsations. He paced up and down the room and then lay on the floor and closed his eyes to meditate, as advised by the healer. No improvement; in fact, his condition worsened.

He finally reconciled that it was time to address the elephant in the room. He had come to Diplomat to do something, but all this while, he was trying to brainwash himself into not doing it. He was dying of heartache, and whatever he was going to do would be an act of self-defence—he reasoned with himself.

The invitation for Gulaabo Night had come with two complimentary bottles of Gulaabo. KD took the two bottles, one in each hand, and knocked at the door at the end of the corridor.

"*Behenchod*, who is it? Just fuck off," a voice boomed from inside.

Instead of replying, KD continued knocking. Finally, after a minute, the door was opened by a person who looked half asleep and half drunk. Before he could react, Dubey broke the bottle on his head. The person fell, and then Dubey broke the second one on his face.

He then took the brass table lamp from the bedside and hit Toni repeatedly until his body became pulp.

He wished Mrs Dubey was there to see the animal in him.

***

By evening, the WhatsApp factory was churning rumours at an alarming rate—'100 people died in Diplomat', 'FLS quota would be increased to 360 ml/day', etc. However, the news that the FLS scheme would be withdrawn at midnight, but all those who had opted for milk instead of liquor would continue to get it for the rest of their lives, caused the FLS website to crash. Many lightweight drinkers rushed to opt for milk, causing the server to crash.

No one knew exactly how many people had entered Diplomat. The optimistic estimate was 20,000, and the pessimistic was about a lakh. The state government had requested additional companies of security forces, but they were yet to arrive. A fuming Siddheshwar Gupta made allegations that the central government was deliberately not sending extra troops to sabotage FLS.

Inside Diplomat, there were scenes of chaos all around. Drunk men were sprawled on the sofas, carpets, tables, floors, and anywhere they could find space. Some were vomiting openly in the fountain at the hotel's lobby. Sanjeev Khanna was the recipient of all the bad news. As such, he was nervous and angry seeing the state of the common areas, but he had a breakdown when it was reported that people had broken open the rooms too.

He immediately activated the hotel's emergency procedures and started a first aid clinic, where Julia could be seen applying balm to the injured. Bika Singh and Rakhi Balwant were among her patients. Their performance had ended before it could begin. Both were molested, and now they shared a bed with a common drip attached to their arms.

Sam Miguel was curled on the floor in the corner of the kitchen sobbing. His kitchen had nothing left. The first few trays of snacks that he had sent to the party were consumed in seconds. The second set never went out because the guests had entered the kitchen by then. They finished all the pakoras, samosas, and even the uncooked foodstuff in the storage, including raw meat. There was a plan to give an ice cream candy to everyone at midnight, coinciding with the implementation of FLS. Leave candy. Not even a stick was left.

Thousands of bottles of Gulaabo were consumed in no time. No one cared for glass—crystal or steel tumbler; they just gulped it from the bottle. To make up for the shortfall, more consignments were dispatched to Diplomat, but most of it was looted midway.

Since morning, Benny had been worried about the safety of the wine cellar in the basement. The cellar had a collection of the choicest whisky, wines, and other such poisons, which were collected over decades for the connoisseur guests of the hotel. A heavy steel door akin to a bank vault guarded the basement. But no obstacle could stop the march of determined drunks. A welding set was lowered, and the cellar was ransacked.

An emergency cabinet meeting was called to assess the situation at Diplomat. It was decided that Gulaabo Night would only be confined to the Royal Salute bar, with only a few VIP invitees. When someone asked about the ordinary people, an angry Siddheshwar Gupta said, "Fuck those assholes. They don't deserve this." He just wanted to get it done with.

At 7.45 pm, tear gas was used to disperse the crowd to ensure the CM's entourage could enter the hotel.

***

In the room adjacent to that of Toni, Moni was missing him. They had not spoken to each other for more than twenty-four hours, a record. Moni didn't want to lose her husband; weren't they made in heaven? She knew exactly what was required to be done. Toni had a legendary libido; the way to his heart was through his dick.

Moni quickly put on her latest shocking red Victoria's Secret lingerie and wore lipstick of the same colour. Satisfied, she covered herself with the bathrobe and walked determinedly towards Toni's room.

***

The CM's car stopped at the porch, and as soon as he got out of the car, he was taken aback by a loud thud. He turned his head towards the direction of the sound. What he saw made his stomach gurgle, and he fell to the ground and started vomiting.

A near naked woman was lying in a pool of blood.

At 8.30 pm, the entire state was engulfed in darkness. There was no duty staff present at the power substations. All were in Diplomat.

***

The Hotel Diplomat had changed a lot over the decades and had somewhat reluctantly shed its colonial heritage. It was now a modern hotel with facilities and services comparable to the best in the world. But despite these changes, the hotel kept some traditions and customs that had become synonymous with its name over the years.

One such tradition was tall guards with giant moustaches at the entrance. They wore a red turban, a red tunic, and a white dhoti. They also carried a hand-held brass shield in one hand and a *bhaala* (javelin) in the other. Though they looked fierce from afar, they had a gentle disposition and smiled and helped every hotel guest.

There were four guards in the current shift. The three had a regular appearance and pleasant disposition, but the fourth one was odd. He was short and stout and aloof. He did not make an attempt to help anyone in the ongoing mayhem and gave an icy stare if anyone tried to approach him. The edges of the *bhaala* carried by the other three guards were blunt, but his had gleaming sharp edges.

When this odd-looking guard saw Siddheshwar lying on the ground and Bhola cleaning his puke, anger swept through his body. At that moment, he learnt that his brother was a *haraami* or, why else, a son of *Kshatriya* would clean someone's vomit? The time had come to finish him.

Banke waited for Siddeshwar Gupta and his entourage to leave and then took a deep breath and charged towards Bhola. Everything happened in a flash. Banke's *bhaala* pierced Bhola's chest, and a millisecond later, Banke received two bullets on his forehead.

Both brothers died in each other's arms.

***

Soundarya Kapoor watched Siddheshwar Gupta slumped on the floor and burst into laughter. She was bordering on drunkenness and didn't flinch when the cameras next panned on Moni's dead body. Instead, she poured herself another drink.

She was running late. As the GCI Chairman and Gulaabo Night's main sponsor, she should have been there to receive the CM; instead, she chose to remain in her room and watch the live action on TV. She simply didn't care because FLS was now a law, and tomorrow, she would sell off the GCI to TWW and start a new life as a lonely but very wealthy widow. She had spoken to the new TWW CEO, and he seemed like a nice man.

The day had been nerve-wracking for her. She had sat watching a live feed of Sumitra Kapoor's target practice the whole day. Her mother-in-law did not know that the one she was planning to hunt was watching her every move, thanks to the webcam installed in her room. She also knew that Tanvi Mehra was the supplier of that gun.

Tanvi Mehra!

Her and Tanvi's destinies were intricately intertwined. If not for Tanvi, she would have never married Kiku and moved to Victoria. If Tanvi had any idea of the consequences of her actions, she would have never done such a thing.

She had been raped in her final year at college, although everyone, including her parents, blamed it on her character. She was Susheela then, a hardworking girl determined to build a career and free herself from the clutches of poverty. Her life revolved around home and college until that fateful night.

It was Tanvi who had forced her to attend the bash. She had reluctantly agreed and sat in a corner the whole time, watching others make merry. Then, at the far end of the party, he approached and offered her a drink. She thought he was safe because he was Tanvi's boyfriend. In hindsight, that made him unsafe, very unsafe.

She had erased that horrid episode from her memory until her rapist had called her earlier in the day she had thrown Tanvi out of M&S. He had cancer and sought penance and told her that Tanvi Mehra was the mastermind behind the whole incident and she was the one who had instigated him. Everyone, including Tanvi, thought she had thrown her out because she got jealous of the success of her birthday party. No. It was because of what had happened twenty years back.

How could one hate another person so much? She was, anyway, much inferior to Tanvi in those days. There was only one explanation—Tanvi was evil. She was a fool to allow Tanvi back into her life.

But then life is strange. Tanvi wanted to finish her, but instead, her life changed for the better after that incident. Not better, but damn good. She had to drop out of college. It was traumatic to face her tormentor every day. To support her family, she did odd jobs until she landed at GCI.

Kiku Kapoor was interning in his own company, and soon, his eyes fell on the introverted girl who kept her head in the accounting files. He was also a shy man, so everything happened slowly. He asked for her help, and she agreed. Every day, she would teach him how to write a ledger. He was also slow and couldn't understand much, but he still sat beside her like an obedient student. She was always kind to him, not that she had an option. He was the heir to the throne. Then, one day, out of the blue, he told her that his parents wanted to meet her.

Soundarya didn't have a decent saree to wear, so Kiku took her in his car and bought her a red chiffon saree. She was explicitly told not to get her parents to the meeting. It was also made clear to her that she would have to abandon her family if she was to marry Kiku. She went alone and cleared the interview in fifteen minutes.

Nothing was asked of her. Only Sumitra Kapoor spoke about how lucky she was and how subservient she had to be for the rest of her life. Embarrassed by his wife's behaviour, Gulab Chand had walked out midway.

A week later, their marriage was conducted in a *mandir* followed by a grand reception at Diplomat in which who's who of Victoria were invited. Again, none of her family members were present at the wedding. In fact, Soundarya never set foot in Azaad Nagar again. Other than occasionally sending money to her family, she took no interest in their lives.

Her father and mother had passed away unexpectedly and quickly during the pandemic, but still, Soundarya gave the cremation a miss. The reality was that she was not, to this day, able to come to terms with her poor background. Her detractors, including her mother-in-law, often pointed at her origins to hurt her, and it stung. She only got Rameshwaram in dowry. Little did she know then that he would become her most potent weapon.

An hour back, Sumitra had asked one of her loyal drivers to take her to Diplomat. The target of the gun in her purse was her daughter-in-law. Little did she realise that the driver's loyalty was questionable under the changed circumstances, and Rameshwaram sat crouched in the Mercedes trunk.

When the driver missed the turn towards Diplomat, Sumitra Kapoor had the first premonition of the danger ahead. However, when it zipped through the *Dhobhi* Colony toll, she became sure that her end was near. Still, she repeatedly hit the driver's shoulders, asking him to turn around. The driver didn't flinch and, after driving for a couple of miles, stopped at a deserted garage. He pressed the switch to open the trunk, and Rameshwaram sprang out.

His instructions were clear. He had to use the hunter's own gun. Before a terrified Sumitra Kapoor could react, he snatched her purse and took out the fully loaded Colt. Then he aimed at her temple.

Her body was disposed of at the *nallah,* an outlet for a million sewers. The flow was strong, and the body became invisible in seconds. When Rameshwaram returned to the car, he saw the urn on the back seat.

"What is to be done with this?" He asked Soundarya on the phone.

"Put it in the same place."

Kiku Kapoor's ashes were immersed in the dirtiest *nallah* in the world.

Soundarya was recalling the events of the day when there was a knock at her door. It was Rameshwaram.

"We have to kill one more snake," she said.

Fifteen minutes later, they proceeded to Royal Salute. She to greet the CM, and he to kill Tanvi Mehra.

***

The sensational escape of the Ghatak gang from the Victoria jail embarrassed the police, and there were demands for the commissioner's resignation. This was new for Nand Kishore, who, throughout his career, had avoided controversies like the plague.

After minutely going through the rules, regulations and protocols, he made his PRO release a cryptic tweet that it was not the commissioner's job to ensure security at the prison, and a show cause notice had been issued to the jailor to provide a detailed investigation report in the next few hours, pending suspension for dereliction of duties.

Inspector Ganpule was leading the search operation. He took it as a personal mission and, in the next few hours, rounded up major and minor criminals for interrogation. Each lawbreaker had a standard response that they had heard of the Ghatak gang and were in awe of what they had done in such a short time.

Still, no one knew much about them except for a pickpocket, who said he was in the same school as Lovely, and it was well known that Lovely always responded disproportionately when he was fingered. He narrated an incident when Lovely had burnt down the scooter of a teacher who had merely asked him to remove his feet from the table.

Meanwhile, the forensic team reported that the explosives used for the blast at the GCI factory were sourced from the notorious Pritam gang of Parbatgunj. Unlike other uneducated criminal gangs, the Pritam gang was known for its scientific temperament and ingenuity in developing complex chemicals and IEDs. In particular, their leader, Pritam Lal, called himself Heisenberg after bingeing on reruns of 'Breaking Bad'. It was vital to catch Pritam to discover Ghatak's next step.

The time was short, so Ganpule and his team rushed to Heisenberg's den. Heisenberg conducted his experiments in the laundry basement, again a choice influenced by the series. Expecting fierce resistance, the SWAT team accompanied the squad as they moved towards the den, but when they reached there, they were surprised that there was no guard and the door was ajar.

The reason for that became apparent as soon as they stepped inside. Heisenberg's laboratory was in shambles. The beakers, jars, and flasks were broken, and chemicals of all kinds were spilt on the floor, emanating such a rancid smell and fumes that everyone had to don the breathing apparatus.

When they cautiously entered the next room, they saw six dead bodies, their faces brutally scalded by razors. Even then, it was easy to identify Heisenberg in his chemist apron. As expected, 'G' was painted on the wall.

Ganpule just stood there, thinking of what the pickpocket had said. Disproportionate response! He had an inkling of what it could be as he rushed towards Diplomat.

***

The sycophants suck up to those on their way up. Politicians are no exception, which was why Tanvi Mehra was the centre of attraction at

Gulaabo Night. She received Siddheshwar Gupta and walked beside him to the Royal Salute amongst the cheering. Whereas Siddheshwar looked dishevelled after witnessing the gruesome suicide, Tanvi walked with her head held high in her starched cotton saree.

Ananya Dutt tweeted the picture of them. "As the old one fades away; a new star is born." In addition to the decision that Gulaabo Night would be confined only to Royal Salute, the program was modified. Now only Victorians were permitted.

Bika and Rakhi Balwant were sick and, in any case, too crude for the select audience, so it was decided that the hotel's in-house band would perform instead, starting with soft jazz and then raising the tempo to coincide with Happy New Year and the roll-out of FLS. It would be a ballroom kind of atmosphere.

The first item on the agenda was raising a toast, and champagne glasses filled with Dom Perignon were given to each guest. Siddheshwar Gupta raised the toast with shaking hands, his mind still on the body outside. He was living his worst nightmare and was contemplating leaving politics altogether. This was not what he had wanted.

The choicest hors d'oeuvre—sushi, salmon, and Pule donkey cheese—were served to the guests. Sanjeev Khanna smiled for the first time in a day. He also called Julia from the staff quarters, "Let someone else take care of the sick fuckers." Julia didn't come alone. With her came Bika Singh and Rakhi Balwant.

They both were openly displaying their newfound affection for each other and, as soon as they entered the Royal Salute, they announced their marriage. In a joint statement to the press members, they said they had left their past animosity behind after facing the life-threatening situation. Then they kissed with open mouths for a good five minutes, making even the biggest perverts red. Bika then broke into a song, praising his manhood.

Tanvi saw Soundarya coming down the transparent elevator. She was wearing a black gown with a plunging neckline that caused the entire Royal Salute to gasp when she made her entry. This annoyed Tanvi to no end. Wasn't she supposed to receive her? She needed to be taught a lesson again. Perhaps the order for FLS should go to some other company. She needed to plan.

Soundarya shook hands with the CM but ignored Tanvi, who was beside the CM. Before she could move away, Tanvi pushed forward and hugged her and whispered in her ears, "Be good to me, bitch, or the order of FLS will go to someone else."

Not to be outdone, Soundarya whispered back, "Be good to me, bitch, or I will kill you." Both women kept staring at each other till the sudden high notes of the band distracted them.

The party's momentum picked up, and soon, soft jazz gave way to hard rock. The couples were jiving, and at one point, the new I&B minister made the press switch off their cameras. These images could not be seen outside.

Sanjeev Khanna was dancing the tango with Julia. Benny was beaming with his eyes on Malaika, who was busy refilling drinks. *Maybe he would get lucky tonight,* he thought and vigorously juggled three bottles of vodka till he dropped all. The M&S gang was enjoying, like always, oblivious to the deaths of Toni and Moni. KD Dubey was slumped at the bar, missing Mrs Dubey and pondering suicide.

The security forces were under tremendous pressure. The public wanted to break open the cordon around Royal Salute. They had become immune to tear gas. Plastic bullets would have only added fuel to the fire.

There was a real danger to the CM's life. There was no liquor in Diplomat other than in the Royal Salute. If people could break in, they would have devoured all the politicians, especially Siddheshwar Gupta.

Ananya Dutt tweeted, "There is a mini-V-AN inside Diplomat. Victorians enjoying at the Royal Salute and Azaad Nagarites struggling outside."

Tanvi Mehra was hobnobbing with a handsome industrialist. She was glad that Toni was not there. Toni was a nuisance, but a drunk Toni was dangerous. She had already blocked his number and unfollowed him on Instagram.

She was discussing her vision as a minister with an ambassador when her phone rang. She ignored it and continued talking, but it rang again. She cursed and took her mobile out to put it in silent mode.

It was then she saw the message from Inspector Ganpule.

Lovely has escaped from jail.

***

Lovely was amazed by the depth of Fattu's father's knowledge of sewers. They had abducted him again, and this time, they wanted to reach the Diplomat. They had considered a stylish kamikaze attack but then realised it was impossible to do that. The crowd outside Diplomat had grown more than five km in radius.

Fattu's father didn't have to be threatened this time. He was sure his son would kill him if he didn't play ball. He marked the start and end sewers on the map and left quietly. The three of them packed their stuff. At 11, the Ghatak gang made their way through a river of shit to reach Diplomat.

***

Tanvi knew she would have to somehow escape. No protection in the world could save her from Lovely. She needed to vanish as soon as possible before he showed up. She made her way towards the ladies room and, on the way, noticed a small passage with a network of pipes. Without giving it a second thought, she entered the passageway.

***

Rameshwaram saw Tanvi going towards the restroom. He followed her and entered the ladies room, but she was not there. In fact, there was no one there. He checked every nook and corner and felt hopeless. What was he going to tell Soundarya? This would be his first failure to let down the only person he had ever loved.

Dejected, he came out, and it was then he saw the narrow passage, and he knew where his prey was hiding. He made his way towards the passage. It was pitch dark, but there was a lot of noise. He switched on his torch and as he moved forward, he saw a large room with all kinds of machinery—generators, air conditioners, boilers, etc.

He started looking for her. Finding her in the darkness was difficult, and after a couple of minutes, he knew there was only one way. He called her mobile. Luckily for him, her phone rang, and Rameshwaram followed the direction of the sound. It took some more time, but finally, he spotted her kneeling behind a machine.

Their eyes met. She was trembling. His instructions were again clear. He had to again use the same gun, the one Tanvi Mehra had given Sumitra Kapoor to kill Soundarya Kapoor. He aimed the gun at her forehead. He was about to squeeze the trigger when he experienced numb fingers.

He collapsed the next second. A bullet was lodged in the back of his head.

***

Soundarya's head was spinning. She felt the same as she had felt many years back at that college party, only that the nausea was more severe. She needed water, but was not able to speak. She unsteadily walked and sat on a vacant sofa.

Normally, Rameshwaram would have come to her rescue, but he was hunting her nemesis at that moment. She could see people she knew, people who admired her and would do anything to be in her good books. But they were all too drunk to notice her sitting in the corner, holding her head. If only someone could give her water.

A few moments later, her wish came true when the girl came to her with a glass. She was the same one who had given her the last drink. She had looked familiar, but now she knew who she was. Kiku had sent her as an agent of her death.

Malaika handed her the glass with a satisfying smile, knowing full well that no amount of water would wash away the poison in Soundarya Kapoor's body.

***

Was she dreaming? She wished so. But one doesn't perceive in dreams, and she could smell the acrid gunpowder. Crushed that it was not a dream, she tried to concentrate first on his fierce face and cold eyes and then on the barrel pointing at her forehead.

Her survival instincts and fear of dying choked her mind with multiple escape plans—talk it out, devise an excuse, make up a story, try seducing him, deliver the performance of her life for the sake of life till she reconciled with reality. There was no point in seeking mercy.

It was game over.

"Kill me," she said and was surprised at the confidence in her own voice. It was as if a part of her was desperate to die.

A few moments passed in which nothing was heard except for the periodic grunt from the exhaust fan's crooked bearing. Six hostile eyes pierced her, but those of Kaalia's were the most hateful.

Would he kill or just hurt her? She was examining his eyes to probe his intentions. She was still looking when he surprisingly spoke softly in a helpless voice, "I cannot kill you because I love you, and I hate myself for it."

She was tempted to blurt—*you fool,* but instead, she looked at him with all the tenderness and kindness she could muster and even managed to emit a few tears. The gangster melted instantly, walked up to her, embraced her, and broke down. She played along, brushing his hair and gently patting his back.

When she said sorry, he declared with teary eyes. "There's nothing more sacred than unrequited love. I set you free."

Fattu and Kaalia were staring at Lovely with astonishment. Although they were in awe of their boss' style, this was a different level. They were unsure if this was the right thing to do because a snake may shed its skin a million times but remains a snake. They wanted to protest but couldn't because the Ghatak gang followed the tenets set by Godfather—*don't take sides against the family members in front of anyone.*

"Leave now," he thundered a few moments later, gesturing to Kaalia to show Tanvi the way through the sewer.

Tanvi looked down at the manhole and was instantly nauseated by the pungent smell and the sight of shit floating and took a step back.

"Don't delay. You may get dirty, but at least you will live because no one else here is going to live," were Lovely's last words to her.

Lovely watched her hurriedly go down the ladder, hoping she would turn to give him one last look.

It is better to be loved and lost. Then never to have loved at all.

She didn't turn.

***

Inspector Ganpule's jeep was caught in the miles-long traffic jam leading up to Diplomat. There was no way he was going to reach there. He tried passing instructions on Motorola, but there was so much noise on the channel because of happenings at Gulaabo Night that his words got lost.

The Diplomat had to be evacuated at any cost. He called Nand Kishore. Nand Kishore heard the ring but ignored it.

Then he received the text—*the hotel needs to be urgently evacuated.*

Again, it was a call to take a decision—the one thing he hated the most. As always, he ignored it. But then he realised that if there was an enquiry later, they would come to know that he had ignored the call for action. It was best to destroy the evidence to be on the safe side.

So, he went to the bathroom and threw his phone in the WC.

Seconds later, the earth shook.

Two Months Later

I lie on the bed all day and stare at the empty wall. Most of the time, I am blank, but sometimes, the lizard on the wall piques my interest. I think she knows all about me, and I feel ashamed when she looks at me like that. Not that she is some saint. I have also seen her attacking her prey with such ruthlessness and passion that I want to tell her that she is not all that different from me. We both are the same.

We all are the same.

Some days, I push myself to go to the balcony, but I can't stay there for more than a few minutes. People are afraid of darkness, but I am afraid of brightness.

I no longer long for my previous life and the things that were the basis of my existence. One can say that the desires in me have ended. I have no connection to the outside world. I dropped my phone during my escape from Diplomat. No one has tried to contact me because I am dead to all.

I have not stepped out of the house for the last two months. The only thing which gave me company and solace was liquor, but I ran out of stock a month back. I cannot get more, not only because I don't have any money, but also because liquor is banned in the state. The punishment for violation is imprisonment.

There are no courts for V-AN so that one could appeal. We are under the president's rule, and the president is very strict. The other day, I learnt from TV that possession of liquor is now treated as a capital offence. Addicts have already left the state, though the president has declared that he would go after all such people and drag them back. According to him, what happened at Diplomat was our collective shame, and we all must repent.

I get withdrawal symptoms and cry. My landlord and Lovely's father sometimes sends food for me, not knowing that he is feeding his son's killer. I look at him from the window. He seems very sad and never opens the paan shop. Lovely's mother has passed away. I saw her dead body from the window.

Nobody comes into my dreams more than Guruji and his calm face. He was so much at peace till I stopped his heartbeat. I sometimes remember Soundarya, too. After all, she was my friend who gave meaning to my life. If she was not there, I would have lived a passionless life like million others. I did spike her drink, but wasn't it for her betterment? If that hadn't happened, she would have ended up as an old hag married to some clerk.

Overall, fifty thousand people died that night. That was the wrath of the Ghatak gang, now regarded as the most brutal gang ever. The investigative agencies are still scratching their heads about how a band of teenagers managed such a large quantity of RDX. I heard in the news that they are making an OTT series on Ghatak. Maybe they should ask me. I was the mother who gave birth to Ghatak.

The Diplomat is nothing but rubble. I still see news of new bodies found every day. They say the president has directed that a spirituality centre should come up at the same site. Spirituality is the new buzzword. They say it is a path to control alcohol cravings. They teach meditation on TV all day. Many spiritual gurus have emerged. I see people sitting on the ground and chanting with their eyes closed.

I also tried it, but it's so fuckin' boring.

Yesterday, I got fed up and asked Lovely's father to call my husband. I desperately want to drink, and maybe Ashok has something with him. My husband is a dependable guy who always saves for rainy days, and this was a rainy day. This morning, he told me that Ashok would come and meet me tonight. It is half-past ten, but he has still not come. There's a probability that he could go to the police. But that was the chance that I had to take.

I am about to give up when I hear a knock. There has been no electricity in the house since last week. FEWS has been withdrawn, and I am penniless to pay the bill. I regret not putting effort into looking decent, though I bathed today after a week. I use a candle to navigate my way to the main door.

There he is. My Ashok. He looks expressionless as always, but I see a bag in his hand, and my excitement grows. He doesn't acknowledge my presence and walks towards the balcony, using his cell phone torch to navigate.

I follow him like a puppy.

He sits on the chair, removes the bottle of Gulaabo from the bag and puts it on the table. He then takes out two glasses.

"I don't have soda," he says suddenly and arrogantly.

"No problem," I say meekly.

He fills up two large pegs and pushes the glass towards me. I hurriedly take a large sip and feel the burn and warmth of the nectar of life.

"So, you did turn the direction of the wheel's rotation."

I keep quiet, not sure if it is a compliment or if he is mocking me. He seems more confident than when I had left him. He also looks slim and better.

"How is your business going?"

"Won't complain; since there is no liquor now, people are spending more on other things and getting their clothes cleaned is one of them."

Once a *dhobhi*, always a *dhobhi*—but I can't dare say that.

He takes out a packet from the bag. I can smell it before he can open it. It's my favourite Chicken Tikka. I attack it. He refills my glass. I notice that he has barely touched his own drink. I gulp the first one, but I am not worried. Ashok is my safe space.

I also gulp the second peg. My mood is lightening. Who said FLS was a sinister scheme? See, just two pegs have made me happy.

"Can you play some music?" I ask him.

He presses a button on his mobile, and Lata's melodious voice fills the air. He knows I like listening to Lata di. He makes my third drink. I suddenly have a rush of affection for him. I go near him and touch his face. I want him to hold me and make me sit on his lap.

He doesn't, and that hurts me. I take out my sweater and then my shirt. He reluctantly fondles my breast, but he is not into me. I pursue more as I place my hand on him. I can now feel the slowly growing warmth in his body.

I light up the cigarette and make another peg. I am confident that he will soon fall for me—once again. Minutes later, he is breathing hard as his body moves up and down. It starts to rain.

For the first time, the enormity of what I did hits me.

Suddenly, I find it hard to breathe. His grip is tightening over my neck.

"Is this the end?"

I sigh silently, and my eyes fall on Gulaabo. Just then, I hear the *Khalnayak* song in my mind and extend my arm to grab the bottle. I know where to aim—half inch above his right eyebrow where the stitches are still raw.